Dedicated to Simon Stannard
and the other victims
of the 26 December 2004 tsunami.
You will not be forgotten.

dear
Nate 'n' Mike
Thank You
      So Much...!!
Goodluck 4 evrything
          GodBless
      George - Shauly

FREDERICK ALLOYSIUS

The Indian Salesman
and other jokes

APHRODITE BAR AND RESTAURANT
Jl. H.R. Rasuna Said Kav. C22
Jakarta 12920

email: fred@aphroditebar.com
web: www.aphroditebar.com

in association with

PT Equinox Publishing Indonesia
www.EquinoxPublishing.com

© 2005 Frederick Alloysius

ISBN 979-3780-05-3

Printed in Indonesia.

All proceeds from the sale of this book will be donated to support the joint initiatives of the Singapore Association in Indonesia, the Singapore Womens Group and the Singapore Embassy towards the rehabilitation of the tsunami victims in Nangro Aceh Darussalam and North Sumatra.

The tsunami of 26 December 2004 affected lots of people in lots of different ways. Dozens of my childhood friends in Nagapatnum and Pondicherry in Tamil Nadu (where I studied for four years) have gone missing or lost their lives. Even Aphrodite was affected – our regular customer and dear friend Simon Stannard of Hill and Associates died while he was on holiday with his family in Khao Lak, Thailand. Simon was a superb man who was on the Aphrodite pool and golf team and was always very kind to everyone he met. Simon, and my friends in Tamil Nadu, will be sorely missed.

I started thinking (yeah, yeah, I know I have been warned about the thinking bit). What could I do to help the victims of this disaster? Our television sets and newspapers are filled with gruesome stories of the more than 150,000 people who died and after a while it gets pretty depressing. After a while, it came to me. What we all need right now is a good laugh.

Most friends of Aphrodite know that I send out a regular email with happenings at Aphrodite and I always include a few jokes at the end. These jokes were sent in from people all over the world and I thought it would be a good idea to compile all of these jokes and make a book out of them – not only to remember Simon but also to help the tsunami victims here in my beloved Indonesia.

I called my good friend Mark Hanusz of Equinox Publishing about the idea to make a book of jokes, and the fact that I needed the book to be ready in a week for the Jakarta Comedy Club benefit show for Simon's family and all of the orphans of the tsunami. After a five-minute discussion, he said "OK, let's do it." We came up with the title "The Indian Salesman and Other Jokes" and the result is what you are now holding in your hands. Thanks for buying it – and in case you don't think the jokes are that funny then just remember that all proceeds from the sales of this book will go to the Singapore Association in Indonesia, the Singapore Womens Group and the Singapore Embassy which will use the funds to help the victims of the tsunami disaster in Aceh.

A word of warning about this book: To have a good laugh, it is sometimes necessary to take the piss out of one another. No offense is intended to any government, race, religion or anything or anyone else for that matter. Some are witty, some are crude, some are slightly off-color but they are jokes and each one will make you laugh (well, they made me laugh at least).

There are many people to thank for their contributions to this book – far to many to name individually. But you know who you are. Thanks to Aphrodite Bar & Restaurant and Equinox Publishing for sponsoring the publication of this book. In particular I'd like to thank Aphrodite's shareholders and my business partner Daniel Gendre as well as the management and staff for all their support. Last but not least, thanks goes to the "Friends of Aphrodite" cardholders and our regular customers.

God bless all of you.

Frederick Alloysius
Jakarta, February 2005

The Indian Salesman
and other jokes

The Indian Salesman

An Indian moves to Montreal and goes to a big department store looking for a job. The manager asks, "Do you have any sales experience?"

The Indian says, "Yeah, I was a salesman back home."

Well, the manager liked the young man, so he gave him the job. "You start tomorrow. I'll come down after we close and see how you did, but let me give you a bit of advice. If a customer comes looking, say, for toothpaste, you might suggest for him a toothbrush, or shaving cream etc. you get the idea?"

"Of course," the young man said. His first day on the job was rough but he got through it.

After the store was locked up, the manager came down. "How many customers did you serve today?"

The Indian says, "One."

The manager groans, "Just one? Our sales people average 20 or 30 sales per day. How much was the sale for?"

The Indian says, "$101,237.64."

The manager exclaims, "What? $101,237.64? What did you sell him?"

The Indian replied, "First I sold him a small fish hook. Then I sold him a medium fishhook. Then I sold him a larger fishhook. Then I sold him a new fishing rod. Then I asked him where he was going fishing, and he said down at the coast, so I told him he was going to need a boat, so we went down to the boat department, and I sold him that twin engine Chris Craft. Then he said he didn't think his Honda Civic would pull it, so I took him down to the automotive department and sold him that 4X4 Pajero."

The manager says "You mean a guy came in here to buy a fish hook and you sold him a boat and truck?!"

The Indian says, "No, no, no, he came in here to buy a box of Kotex for his wife and I said, 'Well, since your weekend's already screwed up you might as well go fishing.'"

Who's That?

Bubba was bragging to his boss one day, "You know, I know everyone there is to know. Just name someone, anyone, and I know them."

Tired of his boasting, his boss called his bluff, "OK, Bubba how about Tom Cruise?"

"Sure, yes, Tom and I are old friends, and I can prove it." So Bubba and his boss fly out to Hollywood and knock on Tom Cruise's door, and sure enough, Tom Cruise, shouts, "Bubba! Great to see you! You and your friend come right in and join me for lunch!"

Although impressed, Bubba's boss is still skeptical. After they leave Cruise's house, he tells Bubba that he thinks Bubba's knowing Cruise was just lucky. "No, no, just name anyone else," Bubba says.

"President Bush," his boss quickly retorts.

"Yes," Bubba says, "I know him, let's fly out to Washington." And off they go. At the White House, Bush spots Bubba on the tour and motions him and his boss over, saying, "Bubba, what a surprise, I was just on my way to a meeting, but you and your friend come on in and let's have a cup of coffee first and catch up."

Well, the boss is very shaken by now, but still not totally convinced. After they leave the White house grounds, he expresses his doubts to Bubba, who again implores him to name anyone else.

"The Pope," his boss replies.

"Sure!" says Bubba. "My folks are from Poland, and

I've known the Pope a long time."

So off they fly to Rome. Bubba and his boss are assembled with the masses in Vatican Square when Bubba says, "This will never work. I can't catch the Pope's eye among all these people. Tell you what, I know all the guards so let me just go upstairs and I'll come out on the balcony with the Pope."

And he disappears into the crowd headed toward the Vatican. Sure enough, half an hour later Bubba emerges with the Pope on the balcony. But by the time Bubba returns, he finds that his boss has had a heart attack and is surrounded by paramedics. Working his way to his boss' side, Bubba asks him, "What happened?"

His boss looks up and says, "I was doing fine until you and the Pope came out on the balcony and the man next to me said, "Who's that on the balcony with Bubba?"

You know you're living in 2005 when...

1. You accidentally enter your password on the microwave.
2. You haven't played solitaire with real cards in years.
3. You have a list of 15 phone numbers to reach your family of 3.
4. You e-mail the person who works at the desk next to you.
7. You make phone calls from home, you accidentally dial "9" to get an outside line.
8. You've sat at the same desk for four years and worked for three different companies.
12. You pull up in your own driveway and use your cell phone to see if anyone is home.
14. Leaving the house without your cell phone, which

you didn't have the first 20 or 30 (or 60) years of your life, is now a cause for panic and you turn around to go and get it.

15. You get up in the morning and go online before getting your coffee.
16. You start tilting your head sideways to smile. :)
17. You're reading this and nodding and laughing.
18. Even worse, you know exactly to whom you are going to forward this message.
19. You are too busy to notice there was no #9 on this list.
20. You actually scrolled back up to check that there wasn't a 9 on this list.

Elementary, My Dear Watson

Sherlock Holmes and Dr. Watson go on a camping trip, set up their tent, and fall asleep. Some hours later, Holmes wakes his faithful friend. "Watson, look up at the sky and tell me what you see."

Watson replies, "I see millions of stars." "What does that tell you?" Watson ponders for a minute. "Astronomically speaking, it tells me that there are millions of galaxies and potentially billions of planets. Astrologically, it tells me that Saturn is in Leo. Timewise, it appears to be approximately a quarter past three. Theologically, it's evident the Lord is all-powerful and we are small and insignificant. Meteorologically, it seems we will have a beautiful day tomorrow. What does it tell you?"

Holmes is silent for a moment, then speaks. "Watson, you idiot, someone has stolen our tent."

Tight Skirt

One day, at a bus stop there was a girl who was wearing a skintight miniskirt. When the bus arrived and it was her turn to get on, she realized that her skirt was so tight she couldn't get her foot high enough to reach to step. Thinking it would give her enough slack to raise her leg, she reached back and unzipped her skirt a little. She still could not reach the step. Embarrassed, she reached back once again to unzip it a little more. Still, she couldn't reach the step. So, with her skirt zipper halfway down, she reached back and unzipped her skirt all the way. Thinking that she could get on the step now, she lifted up her leg only to realize that she still couldn't reach the step. So, seeing how embarrassed the girl was, the man standing behind her put his hands around her waist and lifted her up on to the first step of the bus. The girl turned around furiously and said, "How dare you touch my body that way, I don't even know you!" Shocked, the man says, "Well, ma'am, after you reached around and unzipped my fly three times, I kinda figured that we were friends."

Management Case Study No.1

The manager of a large corporation got a mild heart attack, so his doctor asked him to go to a farm to relax.

The guy went to a farm. And after a couple of days he was very bored, so he asked the farmer to give him some work to do. The farmer asked him to clean the shit of the cattle. The farmer thought that to somebody coming from the city, working the whole life sitting in an office, it would take a week to finish the job. But to his surprise the manager finished it in less than a day.

The next day the farmer gave the manager a more difficult

job and that was to cut the heads of 500 chickens. The farmer was sure the manager would not be able to finish the job in time; but at the end of the day the job was done.

The following morning, the farmer asked the manager to put a bag of potatoes in two boxes: small potatoes in one box and big potatoes in the other. At the end of the day the farmer was surprised to see that the manager was sitting in front of the potato bag, with the two boxes empty.

The farmer asked the manager: "How come you could do difficult jobs in the first two days with ease, but not this simple one?"

The manager answered: "Listen, all through my life I have been dealing with shit and chopping heads, but now you ask me to make decision!"

Management Case Study No.2

A man goes into a pet shop to buy a parrot. The shop owner points to three parrots on a perch and says, "The parrot on the left costs 500 dollars."

"Why does it cost so much?" asks the man.

The shop owner replies, "Well, this parrot knows how to use a computer."

The man then asks about the next parrot to be told that this one costs 1,000 dollars because it can do everything the other parrot can do plus it knows how to use the UNIX operating system.

Naturally, the increasingly startled man asks about the third parrot to be told that it costs 2,000 dollars. Needless to say this begs the question,

"What can it do?"

To which the shop owner replies, "To be honest, I have never seen it do a thing, but the other two call him boss!"

Watch and Learn

Three Indians and three Pakistanis are traveling by train to a cricket match. At the station, the three Pakistanis buy a ticket each and watch as the three Indians buy just one ticket for them all. "How are the three of you going to travel on only one ticket?" asks one of the Pakistanis. "Watch and learn," answers one of the Indians.

They all board the train. The Pakistanis take their respective seats but all three Indians cram into a toilet and close the door behind them. Shortly after the train departs, the conductor comes around collecting tickets. He knocks on the toilet door and says, "Ticket please." The door opens just a crack and a single arm emerges with a ticket in hand. The conductor takes it and moves on. The Pakistanis see this and agree it was quite a clever idea. So, after the game, they decide to copy the Indian style on the return trip and save some money. When they get to the station, they buy one ticket for three on the return trip. To their astonishment, the Indians don't buy ticket at all. "How are you going to travel without a ticket?" says one perplexed Pakistani. "Watch and learn," answers one of the Indiana.

When they board the train, the three Pakistanis quickly cram into one toilet, and soon after the three Indians cram into another nearby toilet. The train departs. Shortly afterwards, one of the Indians leaves the toilet and walks over to the toilet where the Pakistanis are hiding. He knocks on the door and says, "Ticket please." The door opens just a crack and a single arm emerges with a ticket in hand. The Indian takes the ticket and goes back into his toilet.

Drunk Driver

A policeman pulls over a driver for swerving in and out of lanes on the highway. He tells the guy to blow a breath into a breathalyzer.

"I can't do that, officer."

"Why not?"

"Because I'm an asthmatic. I could get an asthma attack if I blow into that tube."

"Okay, we'll just get a urine sample down at the station."

"Can't do that either, officer."

"Why not?"

"Because I'm a diabetic. I could get low blood sugar if I pee in a cup."

"Alright, we could get a blood sample."

"Can't do that either, officer."

"Why not?"

"Because I'm a hemophiliac. If I give blood I could die."

"Fine then, just walk this white line."

"Can't do that either, officer."

"Why not?"

"Because I'm drunk."

Conversion

A Catholic priest, a Pentecostal preacher and a Muslim kyai all served as chaplains to the students of a University in Marquette, USA. They would get together two or three times a week for coffee and to talk shop.

One day, someone made the comment that preaching to people isn't really that hard. A real challenge would be to preach to a bear. One thing led to another, and they decided to do a seven-day experiment. They would all go out into the woods, find a bear and preach to it.

Seven days later, they're all together to discuss the experience. Father O'Flannery, who has his arm in a sling, is on crutches, and has various bandages, goes first.

"Wellll," he says, in a fine Irish brouge, "Ey wint oot into th' wooods to fynd me a bearr. Oond when Ey fund him Ey began to rread to him from the Baltimorre Catechism. Welll, thet bearr wanted naught to do wi' me und begun to slap me aboot. So I quick grrabbed me holy water and, THE SAINTS BE PRAISED, he became as gentle as a lamb. The bishop is cooming oot next wik to give him fierst communion und confierrmation."

Reverend Billy Bob spoke next. He was in a wheelchair, with an arm and both legs in casts, and an IV drip. In his best fire and brimstone oratory he proclaimed, "WELL, brothers, you KNOW that we don't sprinkle...WE DUNK! I went out and I FOUND me a bear. And then I began to read to him from God's HOOOOLY WORD! But that bear wanted nothing to do with me. I SAY NO! He wanted NOTHING to do with me. So I took HOOOLD of him and we began to rassle. We rassled down one hill, UP another and DOWN another until we come to a crick. So I quick DUNK him and BAPTIZE his hairy soul. An' jus like you sez, he wuz gentle as a lamb. We spent the rest of the week in fellowship, feasting on God's HOOOOLY word."

They both look down at the Kyai Hasan, who was lying in a hospital bed. He was in a body cast and traction with IV's and several equipment and monitors running in and out of him.

The kyai looks up and says, "Oy! You don't know what TOUGH is until you try to circumcise one of those creatures."

Praying Parrots

A lady goes to her priest one day and tells him, "Father, I have a problem. I have two female parrots, but they only know how to say one thing."

What do they say?" the priest inquired.

They say, "Hi, we're hookers! Do you want to have some fun?"

That's obscene!" the priest exclaimed. Then he thought for a moment. "You know," he said, "I may have a solution to your problem. I have two male talking parrots, which I have taught to pray and read the Bible. Bring your two parrots over to my house, and we'll put them in the cage with Francis and Job. My parrots can teach your parrots to praise and worship and your parrots are sure to stop saying ...that phrase...in no time."

Thank you," the woman responded, "this may very well be the solution."

The next day, she brought her female parrots to the priest's house. As he ushered her in, she saw that his two male parrots were inside their cage, holding rosary beads and praying. Impressed, she walked over and placed her parrots in with them.

After a few minutes, the female parrots cried out in unison: "Hi, we're hookers! Do you want to have some fun?"

There was stunned silence. Shocked, one male parrot looked over at the other male parrot and exclaimed, "Put the beads away, Frank. Our prayers have been answered!"

Revenge

A woman walks into a drugstore and asks the druggist for some arsenic. The druggist asks "Ma'am, what do you want with arsenic?" "To kill my husband." "I'm sorry Ma'am, I can't sell you any for that reason." The woman then hands him a photo of a man and a woman in a compromising position. The man is her husband, and the woman is the druggist's wife. He looks at the photo and says, "My apologies, I didn't realize you had a prescription."

Why Condi is Secretary of State

George: Condi! Nice to see you. What's happening?

Condi: Sir, I have the report here about the new leader of China.

George: Great. Lay it on me.

Condi: Hu is the new leader of China.

George: That's what I want to know.

Condi: That's what I'm telling you.

George: That's what I'm asking you. Who is the new leader of China?

Condi: Yes.

George: I mean the fellow's name.

Condi: Hu.

George: The guy in China.

Condi: Hu.

George: The new leader of China.

Condi: Hu.

George: The Chinaman!

Condi: Hu is leading China.

George: Now whaddya' asking me for?

Condi: I'm telling you Hu is leading China.

George: Well, I'm asking you. Who is leading China?

Condi: That's the man's name.

George: That's who's name?

Condi: Yes.

George: Will you or will you not tell me the name of the new leader of China?

Condi: Yes, sir.

George: Yassir? Yassir Arafat is in China? The guy from the Middle East? I thought he just died?

Condi: That's correct.

George: Then who is in China?

Condi: Yes, sir.

George: Yassir is in China?

Condi: No, sir.

George: Then who is?

Condi: Yes, sir.

George: Yassir?

Condi: No, sir.

George: Look, Condi. I need to know the name of the new leader of China. Get me the Secretary General of the U.N. on the phone.

Condi: Kofi?

George: No, thanks.

Condi: You want Kofi?

George: No.

Condi: You don't want Kofi?

George: No. But now that you mention it, I could use a glass of milk . . . and then get me the U.N.

Condi: Yes, sir.

George: Not Yassir! The guy at the U.N.

Condi: Kofi?

George: Milk! Will you please make the call?

Condi: And call who?

George: Who is the guy at the U.N?

Condi: Hu is the guy in China.

George: Will you stay out of China?!

Condi: Yes, sir.

George: And stay out of the Middle East! Just get me the guy at the U.N.

Condi: Kofi.

George: All right! With cream and two sugars. Now get on the phone.

(Condi picks up the phone.)

Condi: Rice, here.

George: Rice? Good idea. And a couple of egg rolls, too. Maybe we should send some to the guy in China. And the Middle East. Can you get Chinese food in the Middle East?

Engineering in Hell

An engineer dies and reports to the pearly gates. St. Peter checks his dossier and says, "Ah, you're an engineer – you're in the wrong place." So, the engineer reports to the gates of hell and is let in. Pretty soon, the engineer gets dissatisfied with the level of comfort in hell, and starts designing and building improvements. After awhile, they've got air conditioning and flush toilets and escalators, and the engineer is a pretty popular guy.

One day, God calls Satan up on the telephone and says with a sneer, "So, how's it going down there in hell?" Satan replies, "Hey, things are going great. We've got air conditioning and flush toilets and escalators, and there's no telling what this engineer is going to come up with next." God replies, "What??? You've got an engineer? That's a mistake – he should never have gotten down there; send him up here." Satan says, "No way." I like having an engineer on the staff, and I'm keeping him." God says, "Send him back up here or I'll sue." Satan laughs uproariously and answers, "Yeah, right. And just where are YOU going to get a lawyer?"

What is Marketing?

You see a gorgeous girl at a party. You go up to her and say, "I am very rich. Marry me!" That's Direct Marketing

You're at a party with a bunch of friends and see a gorgeous girl. One of your friends goes up to her and pointing at you says, He's very rich. Marry him." That's Advertising.

You see a gorgeous girl at a party. You go up to her and get her telephone number. The next day you call and say, "Hi, I'm very rich. Marry me." That's Telemarketing.

You're at a party and see a gorgeous girl. You get up and straighten your tie; you walk up to her and pour her a drink. You open the door for her, pick up her bag after she drops it, offer her a ride, and then say, "By the way, I'm very rich "Will you marry me?" That's Public Relations.

You're at a party and see a gorgeous girl. She walks up to you and says, "You are very rich, I want to marry you." That's Brand Recognition.

You see a gorgeous girl at a party. You go up to her and say, "I'm rich. Marry me." She gives you a nice hard slap on your face. That's Customer Feedback.

It's a Tragedy

John Kerry visits a primary school classroom. They are in the middle of a discussion related to words and their meanings. The teacher asks Mr. Kerry if he would like to lead the discussion on the word "tragedy." So the illustrious Senator asks the class for an example of a tragedy. One little boy stands up and offers: "If my best friend, who lives on a farm, is playing in the field and a tractor runs him over and kills him that would be a 'tragedy'."

"No," says Kerry, "that would be an 'accident'."

A little girl raises her hand: "If a school bus carrying 50 children drove over a cliff, killing everyone inside, that would be a tragedy."

"I'm afraid not," explains Mr. Kerry. "That's what we would call a 'great loss'."

The room goes silent. No other children volunteered. Kerry searches the room. "Isn't there someone here who can give me an example of a 'tragedy'?" Finally, at the back of the room a small boy raises his hand. In a quiet voice, he says: "If your campaign plane, carrying you, Mr. Kerry, were struck by a 'friendly fire' missile and blown to smithereens that would be a 'tragedy'."

"Fantastic!" exclaims Kerry. "That's right. And can you tell me why that would be a 'tragedy'?"

"Well," says the boy "because it certainly wouldn't be a 'great loss' and it probably wouldn't be an 'accident' either."

Drunk in Church
A drunk staggers into a church, enters a confessional booth, sits down but says nothing. The priest coughs a few times to get his attention but the drunk just sits there. Finally, the priest pounds three times on the wall. The drunk mumbles, "ain't no use knockin', there's no paper on this side either."

That's Not What I Meant
A fairy told a married couple: "For being such an exemplary married couple for 35 years, I will give you each a wish."

"I want to travel around the world with my dearest husband," said the wife.

The fairy moved her magic wand and - abracadabra! - two tickets appeared in her hands. Now it was the husband's turn. He thought for a moment and said: "Well this moment is very romantic, but an opportunity like this only occurs once in a lifetime. So...I'm sorry my love, but my wish is to have a wife 30 years younger than me."

The wife was deeply disappointed but, a wish was a wish. The fairy made a circle with her magic wand and - abracadabra! Suddenly the husband was 90 years old.

Dead Goldfish

Little Tim was in the garden filling a hole when his neighbor peered over the fence. Interested in what the cheeky-faced youngster was up to, he politely asked, "What are you up to there, Tim?"

"My goldfish died," replied Tim tearfully, without looking up, "and I've just buried him."

The neighbor said, "That's an awfully big hole for a goldfish, isn't it, Tim?"

Tim patted down the last heap of earth and replied, "That's because I couldn't get him out of your cat."

The Offer

A young girl missed her period for two months. Very worried, the mother goes to the drugstore and buys a pregnancy kit. The test result shows that the girl is pregnant.

Shouting, cursing, crying, the mother says, "Who was the pig that did this to you? I want to know!"

The girl picks up the phone and makes a call. Half an hour later a Ferrari stops in front of their house; a mature and distinguished man with gray hair and impeccably dressed in a very expensive suit steps out of it and enters the house.

He sits in the living room with the father, the mother and the girl, and tells them: "Good morning, your daughter has informed me of the problem. However, I can't marry her because of my personal family situation, but I'll take responsibility. "If a girl is born I will bequeath her 2 retail stores, a townhouse, a beach villa and a $1,000,000 bank account. If a boy is born, my legacy will be a couple of factories and a $2,000,000 bank account. If it is twins, a factory and $1,000,000 each. However, if there is a miscarriage, what do you suggest I do?"

At this point, the father, who had remained silent, places a hand firmly on the man's shoulder and tells him, "You can try again!"

Raw Materials

In school one day the teacher decided in science class she would teach about materials. So she stood in the front of the class and said, "Children, if you could have one raw material in the world what would it be?"

Little Ritchie raised his hand and said "I would want gold; because gold is worth a lot of money and I could buy a Porsche."

The teacher nodded and called on little Susie Marie.

Little Susie said "I would want platinum because platinum is worth more than gold and I could buy a Corvette."

The teacher smiled and then called on Little Johnny. Little Johnny stood up and said, "I would want silicone."

The teacher said, "Why Johnny?"

He responded by saying, "Because my mom has two bags of it and you should see all the sports cars outside our house!!"

What happened?

This guy wakes up at home with a huge hangover. He forces himself to open his eyes, and the first thing he sees is a couple of aspirin and glass of water on the side table. He sits up and sees his clothing in front of him, all clean and pressed. He looks around the room and sees that it is in a perfect order, spotless clean, and so is the rest of the house.

He takes the aspirin and notices a note on the table. "Honey, breakfast is on the stove. Love you." So he goes to the kitchen and sure enough there is a hot breakfast, fresh newspaper. His son is also at the table, eating.

Father: "Son, what happened yesterday?"

Son: "Oh, the usual. You came home after 3 am, drunk and delirious. Broke some furniture, puked in the hallway, usual stuff."

Father: "So, why is everything in order and so clean, and the food is on the table?"

Son: "Oh that! Mom dragged you to the bedroom, and when she tried to take your pants off you said, "Leave me alone bitch! I'm married!"

Going Shopping

This happens at a country club. A handphone on a bench rings and a man engages the hands-free speaker function and begins to talk. Everyone else in the room stops to listen.

MAN: "Hello"

WOMAN: "Honey, it's me. Are you at the club?"

MAN: "Yes"

WOMAN: "I am at the mall now and found this beautiful leather coat. It's only £1,000. Is it OK if I buy it?"

MAN: "Sure ... go ahead if you like it that much."

WOMAN: "I also stopped by the Mercedes dealership and saw the new 2005 models. I saw one I really liked."

MAN: "How much?"

WOMAN: "£60,000"

MAN: "OK, but for that price I want it with all the options."

WOMAN: "Great! Oh, and one more thing...the house we wanted last year is back on the market. They're asking £950,000."

MAN: "Well, then go ahead and give them an offer, but just offer £900,000"

WOMAN: "OK. I'll see you later. I love you!"

MAN: "Bye, I love you, too."

The man hangs up. The other men in the locker room are looking at him in astonishment. Then he asks: "Anyone know who this phone belongs to?"

Killing Flies

A housewife walked into her kitchen to see her husband with a flyswatter in his hand. She asked, "Honey, what are you doing?"

He responded, "Oh, just swatting flies."

She asked. "Killing any?"

He responded, "Yes, got 3 males and 2 females!"

"Good", she said, and turned to walk away. But then a puzzling thought overcame her and she turned back towards her husband and asked, "Honey, how could you tell the sex of the flies?"

He responded, "Well, 3 were on the beer can and 2 were on the phone."

Don't Eat It

A hunter kills a deer and brings it home. He decides to clean it, prepare it, and serve the deer meat for dinner. He knows his kids are fussy eaters, and won't eat it if they know what it is, so he doesn't tell them. His little boy keeps asking him, "What's for dinner dad?"

"You'll see", he replies. They start eating dinner and his daughter keeps asking him what they are eating.

"OK," says her dad. "Here's a hint. It's what your mother sometimes calls me."

His daughter screams, "Don't eat it, Jimmy! It's a fucking asshole!"

Studying Hard

Little Zachary, a Jewish kid, was doing very badly in math. His parents had tried everything: tutors, mentors, flash cards, special learning centers, in short, everything they could think of to help his math!

Finally, in a last ditch effort, they took Zachary down and enrolled him in the local Catholic school. After the first day, little Zachary came home with a very serious look on his face. He didn't even kiss his mother hello. Instead, he went straight to his room and started studying. Books and papers were spread out all over the room and little Zachary was hard at work.

His mother was amazed. She called him down to dinner, to her shock, the minute he was done, he marched back to his room without a word, and in no time, he was back hitting the books as hard as before. This went on for some time, day after day while the mother tried to understand what made all the difference. Finally, little Zachary brought home his report card. He quietly laid it on the table, went up to his room, and hit the books.

With great trepidation, his Mom looked at it and to her great surprise, little Zachary got an "A" in math. She could no longer hold her curiosity. She went to his room and said: "Son, what was it? Was it the nuns?" Little Zachary looked at her and shook his head, no. "Well, then," she replied, "was it the books, the discipline, the structure, the uniforms? WHAT was it?" Little Zachary looked at her and said, "Well, on the first day of school, when I saw that guy nailed to the plus sign, I knew they weren't fucking around."

Potentially vs. Reality

Youngest son: "Tell me Daddy, what is the difference between 'potentially' and 'in reality'?"

Dad: "I will show you." Dad turns to his wife and asks her: "Would you sleep with Robert Redford for 1 million dollars?"

Wife: "Yes of course, I would never waste such an opportunity!"

Then Dad asks his daughter if she would sleep with Brad Pitt for 1 million dollars.

Daughter: "Wow! Oh my God!!! This is my fantasy!"

So Dad turns to his elder son and asks him: "Would you sleep with Tom Cruise for 1 million dollars?"

Elder Son: "Huh, yeah, why not? Imagine what I could do with 1 million dollars! I wouldn't even hesitate!"

So the father turns back to his younger son saying: "You see son, 'potentially' we are sitting on 3 million dollars, but 'in reality' we are living with 2 whores and 1 gay!"

The Birds and the Bees

A father asked his son, Little Johnny, if he knew about the birds and the bees. "I don't want to know!" Little Johnny said, bursting into tears. Confused, his father asked Little Johnny what was wrong. "Oh Pop," Johnny sobbed, "For me there was no Santa Claus at age six, no Easter Bunny at seven, and no Tooth Fairy at eight. And if you're telling me now that grownups don't really have sex, I've got nothing left to believe in!"

Missing Sugar Bowl

A mother comes to visit her son Anthony for dinner, who lives with a female roommate named Vikki. During the course of the meal, his mother couldn't help but notice how pretty Anthony's roommate was. She had long been suspicious of a relationship between the two, and this had only made her more curious. Over the course of the evening, while watching the two interact, she started to wonder if there was more between Anthony and his roommate. Reading his mom's thoughts, Anthony volunteered, "I know what you must be thinking, but I assure you, Vikki and I are just roommates."

About a week later, Vikki came to Anthony saying, "Ever since your mother came to dinner, I've been unable to find the silver sugar bowl. You don't suppose she took it, do you?" Well, I doubt it, but I'll email her, just to be sure." So he sat down and wrote:

Dear Mama, I'm not saying that you 'did' take the sugar bowl from my house, I'm not saying that you 'did not' take it. But the fact remains that it has been missing ever since you were here for dinner. Love, Anthony

Several days later, Anthony received a response email from his Mama, which read:

Dear Son, I'm not saying that you 'do' sleep with Vikki, and I'm not saying that you 'do not' sleep with her. But the fact remains that if she were sleeping in her OWN bed, she would have found the sugar bowl by now. Love, Mama

Dry Cleaning

Two buddies, Jeff and Steve, are getting very drunk at a bar when suddenly Jeff throws up all over himself. "Oh, no, Jane will kill me!"

Steve says, "Don't worry, pal. Just tuck a twenty in your breast pocket and tell Jane that someone threw up on you and gave you twenty dollars for the dry cleaning bill."

So they stay for another couple hours and get even more drunk. Eventually Jeff rolls into home and Jane starts to give him a hard time.

"You reek of alcohol and you puked all over yourself! My God you are disgusting!"

Speaking very carefully so as not to slur, Jeff says, "Nowainaminit, I can e'splain everything! Ish not what you thinks, I only had a couple drinks! But this other guy got sick on me...he'd had one too many and couldn't hold his liquor! He said he was sorry an' gave me $20 for the cleaning bill!"

Jane looks in his breast pocket, "But this is forty dollars!"

"Oh yeah," says Jeff, "I almost forgot! Hess shit in my pants too!"

Smart Kid

A little kid walks into a city bus and sits right behind the driver and starts yelling, "If my dad was a bull and my mom a cow I'd be a little bull." The driver starts getting mad at the noisy kid, who continues with, "If my dad was an elephant and my mom a girl elephant I would be a little elephant." The kid goes on with several animals until the bus driver gets angry and yells at the kid, "What if your dad was a drunk and your mom was a prostitute?" The kid smiles and says, "I would be a bus driver!"

The Conductor

A mother was working in the kitchen, listening to her five-year-old son playing with his new electric train in the living room. She heard the train stop and her son saying, "All you bastards who want off, get the hell off now, 'cause this is the last stop! And all you bastards who are getting on, get your ass in the train, 'cause we're going down the tracks."

The horrified mother went in and told her son, "We don't use that kind of language in this house. Now I want you to go to your room and stay there for TWO HOURS. When you come out, you may play with your train, but I want you to use nice language."

Two hours later, the son came out of the bedroom and resumed playing with his train. Soon the train stopped and the mother heard her son say, "All passengers who are disembarking the train, please remember to take all your belongings with you. We thank you for traveling with us today & hope your trip was a pleasant one."

She heard the little boy continue, "For those of you just boarding, we ask you to stow all your hand luggage under your seat. Remember, there is no smoking on the train. We hope you will have a pleasant and relaxing journey with us today."

As the mother began to smile, the child added, "For those of you who are pissed off about the TWO-HOUR delay, please direct your complaints to the fat bitch in the kitchen. Thank you for traveling with us."

Baby Food

A three-year-old walked up to a pregnant lady while waiting with his mother in the doctor's office. He inquisitively asked the lady, "Why is your stomach so big?"

She replied, "I'm having a baby."

With big eyes, he asked, "Is the baby in your stomach?"

She answered, "He sure is."

Then the little boy, with a puzzled look, asked, "Is it a good baby?"

She said, "Oh, yes. It's a real good baby."

With an even more surprised and shocked look, he asked, "Then why did you eat him?"

I'd Rather Have a Puppy

A little boy and his dad were walking down the street when they saw two dogs having sex. The little boy asks his father "Daddy, what are they doing?" The father says, "Making a puppy" So they walk on and go home.

A few days later, the little boy walks in on his parents having sex.

The little boy says "Daddy, what are you doing?"

The father replies, "Making a baby."

The little boy says "Hmmmm, can you please flip Mommy around? I'd rather have a puppy instead!"

Smart Baby

A baby was born so advanced in development he could talk. He looked around the delivery room and saw the doctor. "Are you my doctor?" he asked.

"Why, yes, I am," said the doctor.

The baby said, "Thank you for taking such good care of me during the birth."

He looked at his mother and asked, "Are you my mother?"

"Yes, dear, I am," said the mother, beaming.

"Thank you for taking such good care of me before I was born," he said.

He then looked at his father and asked, "Are you my father?"

"Yes, I am," his father proudly answered. The baby motioned him closer, then poked him repeatedly on the forehead with his index finger. "Hurts, doesn't it!?"

Gorilla on my Roof

A man wakes up one morning to find a gorilla on his roof. So he looks in the yellow pages and sure enough, there's an ad for Gorilla Removers. He calls the number, and the gorilla remover says he'll be over in minutes. The gorilla remover arrives, and gets out of his van. He's got a ladder, a baseball bat, a shotgun and a mean old pit bull. "What are you going to do?" the homeowner asks.

"I'm going to put this ladder up against the roof, and then I'm going to go up there and knock the gorilla off the roof with this baseball bat. When the gorilla falls off, the pit bull is trained to grab his testicles and not let go. The gorilla then will be subdued enough for me to put him in the cage in the back of the van."

He hands the shotgun to the homeowner. "What's the shotgun for? asks the homeowner."

"If the gorilla knocks me off the roof, shoot the damn dog!"

Lucky Frog

A man takes the day off work and decides to go out golfing. He is on the second hole when he notices a frog sitting next to the green. He thinks nothing of it and is out to shoot when he hears, Ribbit 9 Iron."

The man looks around and doesn't see anyone. Again, he hears, "Ribbit 9 Iron." He looks at the frog and decides to prove the frog wrong, puts the club away, and grabs a 9 iron. Boom! He hits it 10 inches from the cup. He is shocked. He says to the frog, "Wow that's amazing. You must be a lucky frog, eh?

The frog replies, "Ribbit Lucky frog."

The man decides to take the frog with him to the next hole. "What do you think frog?" the man asks. "Ribbit 3 wood." The guy takes out a 3 wood and, Boom! Hole in one. The man is befuddled and doesn't know what to say. By the end of the day, the man golfed the best game of golf in his life and asks the frog, "OK where to next?" The frog replies, "Ribbit Las Vegas."

They go to Las Vegas and the guy says, "OK frog, now what?" The frog says, "Ribbit Roulette." Upon approaching the roulette table, The man asks, "What do you think I should bet?" The frog replies, "Ribbit $3000, black 6."

Now, this is a million-to-one shot to win, but after the golf game the man figures what the heck. Boom! Tons of cash comes sliding back across the table. The man takes his winnings and buys the best room in the hotel. He sits the frog down and says, "Frog, I don't know how to repay you. You've won me all this money and I am forever grateful." The frog replies, "Ribbit Kiss Me." He figures why not, since after all the frog did for him, he deserves it. With a kiss, the frog turns into a gorgeous 15-year-old girl.

"And that, your honor, is how the girl ended up in my room."

Peckers

A Georgia woodpecker and a Kentucky woodpecker were arguing about which state had the toughest trees. The Georgia woodpecker said that they had a tree that no woodpecker could peck. The Kentucky woodpecker challenged him and promptly pecked a hole in the tree with no problem.

The Georgia woodpecker was in awe. The Kentucky woodpecker then challenged the Georgia woodpecker to peck a tree in Kentucky that was absolutely un-peckable. The Georgia woodpecker expressed confidence that he could do it and accepted the challenge. After flying to Kentucky, the Georgia woodpecker successfully pecked the tree with no problem. The two woodpeckers were now confused.

How is it that the Kentucky woodpecker was able to peck the Georgia tree and the Georgia woodpecker was able to peck the Kentucky tree when neither one was able to peck the tree in their own state? After much woodpecker pondering, they both came to the same conclusion:

Your pecker is always harder when you're away from home.

Wartime Camel

The new American Marine Captain was assigned to a Irish Regiment in a remote post in the Lebanese desert. During his first inspection, he noticed a camel hitched up behind the mess tent. He asks the Irish Sergeant why the camel is kept there. "Well, sir," is the nervous reply, "As you know, there are 250 men here and no women. And sir, sometimes the men have ...m-m-m.... urges. That's why we have the camel, sir."

The American Captain says, "I can't say that I condone this, but I understand about urges, so the camel can stay."

About a month later, the Captain starts having a real problem with his own urges. Crazy with passion, he asks the Irish Sergeant to bring the camel to his tent. Putting a stool behind the camel, the Captain stands on it, pulls down his pants, and has wild, insane sex with the camel.

When he is done, he asks the Sergeant, "Is that how the Irish do it?"

"Uh, no sir," the Sergeant replies. "They usually just ride the camel into town where the girls are."

Pack a Bottle Opener

Three tortoises, Troy, Andy and Wayne, decide to go on a picnic. Troy packs the picnic basket with beer and sandwiches. The trouble is that the picnic site is ten miles away so it takes them ten days to get there. When they get there, Troy unpacks the food and beer and says "Ok Wayne give me the bottle opener."

"I didn't bring it," says Wayne

"I thought you packed it."

Troy gets worried, He turns to Andy, "Did you bring the bottle opener?"

Naturally Andy didn't bring it. So they're stuck ten miles from home without a bottle opener. Troy and Andy beg Wayne to go back for it. But he refuses as he says they will eat all the sandwiches. After two hours, and after they have sworn on their tortoise lives that they will not eat the sandwiches, he finally agrees. So Wayne sets off down the road at a steady pace.

Twenty days pass and he still isn't back and Troy and Andy are starving, but a promise is a promise. Another 5 days and he still isn't back, but a promise is a promise. Finally they can't take it any longer so they take out a sandwich each, and just as they are about to eat them, Wayne pops up from behind a rock and shouts, "I knew it! I'm not fucking going!"

Christmas Present

At Christmas, a little girl goes to see Santa. She climbs on his lap and smiles.

Santa says," And what can I bring you for Christmas?"

The little girl says, " I want a Barbie and a GI Joe."

Santa looks at her and says," I thought Barbie comes with Ken."

The little girl says, "No, Barbie comes with GI Joe, she fakes it with Ken."

Getting into Heaven

Three men died on Christmas Eve and were met by Saint Peter at the Pearly Gates. "In honor of this holy season," Saint Peter said, "you must each possess something that symbolizes Christmas to get into heaven."

The first man fumbled through his pockets and pulled out a lighter. He flicked it on." It represents a candle," he said.

"You may pass through the Pearly Gates," Saint Peter said.

The second man reached into his pocket and pulled out a set of keys. He shook them and said, "They're bells." Saint Peter said "You may pass through the Pearly Gates.

The third man started searching desperately through his pockets and finally pulled out a pair of women's panties. St. Peter looked at the man with a raised eyebrow and asked, "And just what do those symbolize?"

The man replied, "They're Carol's."

Don't Mess with Santa

One particular Christmas season a long time ago, Santa was getting ready for his annual trip but there were problems everywhere. Four of his elves got sick, and the trainee elves did not produce the toys as fast as the regular ones so Santa was beginning to feel the pressure of being behind schedule. Then Mrs. Claus told Santa that her mom was coming to visit.

This stressed Santa even more. When he went to harness the reindeer, he found that three of them were about to give birth and two had jumped the fence and were out, heaven knows where. More stress.

Then when he began to load the sleigh one of the boards cracked and the toy bag fell to the ground and scattered the toys. So, frustrated, Santa went into the house for a cup of coffee and a shot of whiskey. When he went to the cupboard, he discovered that the elves had hid the liquor and there was nothing to drink. In his frustration, he accidentally dropped the coffee pot and it broke into hundreds of little pieces all over the kitchen floor.

He went to get the broom and found that mice had

eaten the straw it was made from. Just then the doorbell rang and Santa cussed on his way to the door. He opened the door and there was a little angel with a great big Christmas tree.

The angel said, very cheerfully, "Merry Christmas Santa! Isn't it just a lovely day? I have a beautiful tree for you. Isn't it just a lovely tree? Where would you like me to stick it?"

Thus began the tradition of the little angel on top of the Christmas tree.

Smart Computer

One day, in line at the company cafeteria, Jack says to Mike behind him, "My elbow hurts like hell. I guess I better see a doctor."

"Listen, you don't have to spend that kind of money," Mike replies. "There's a diagnostic computer down at Wal-Mart. Just give it a urine sample and the computer will tell you what's wrong and what to do about it. It takes ten seconds and costs ten dollars...a lot cheaper than a doctor." So Jack deposits a urine sample in a small jar and takes it to Wal-Mart. He deposits ten dollars, and the computer lights up and asks for the urine sample. He pours the sample into the slot and waits. Ten seconds later, the computer ejects a printout:

```
You have tennis elbow. Soak your arm
in warm water and avoid heavy activity.
It will improve in two weeks.
```

That evening while thinking how amazing this new technology was, Jack began wondering if the computer could be fooled. He mixed some tap water, a stool sample from his dog, urine samples from his wife and daughter, and masturbated into the mixture for good measure. Jack hurries back to Wal-Mart, eager to check the results. He deposits ten dollars, pours in his concoction, and awaits the results.

The computer prints the following:

1. Your tap water is too hard. Get a water softener.
2. Your dog has ringworm. Bathe him with anti-fungal shampoo.
3. Your daughter has a cocaine habit. Get her into rehab.
4. Your wife is pregnant. Twins. They aren't yours. Get a lawyer.
5. If you don't stop playing with yourself, your elbow will never get better.

Thank you for shopping at Wal-Mart.

Pick One

A Marine stationed in Afghanistan recently received a "Dear John" letter from his girlfriend back home. It read as follows:

Dear Ricky, I can no longer continue our relationship. The distance between us is just too great. I must admit that I have cheated on you twice, since you've been gone, and it's not fair to either of us. I'm sorry. Please return the picture of me that I sent to you. Love, Becky

The Marine, with hurt feelings, asked his fellow Marines for any snapshots they could spare of their girlfriends, sisters, ex-girlfriends, aunts, cousins etc. In addition to the picture of Becky, Ricky included all the other pictures of the pretty gals he had collected from his buddies. There were 57 photos in that envelope...along with this note:

Dear Becky, I'm so sorry, but I can't quite remember who the fuck you are. Please take your picture from the pile, and send the rest back to me. Take Care, Ricky

Lessons to Learn

A man took his wife to the rodeo and one of the exhibits is that of breeding bulls. They went up to the first pen and there was a sign that said, "This bull mated 50 times last year." The wife poked her husband in the ribs and said, "He mated 50 times last year." They walked a little further and saw another pen with a sign that said, "This bull mated 120 times last year." The wife hit her husband and said, "That's more than twice a week! You could learn a lot from him.

They walked further and a third pen had a bull with a sign saying, "This bull mated 365 times last year." The wife got really excited and said, "That's once a day. You could REALLY learn something from this one."

The husband looked at her and said, "Go up and ask him if it was with the same cow."

The husband's condition has been reduced from critical to stable and he should make a full recovery.

Letter to Alcohol

Dear Alcohol,
I have been staying away from you for about 10 days now and I thought I'd take a minute to discuss some troubling factors with you before I start with you again.

First and foremost, let me tell you that I'm a huge fan of yours. Your many sides and dimensions are mind-boggling (different than beer goggling, which I'll touch upon shortly.) Yes, my friend, you always seem to be there when needed: the perfect post-work cocktail, a beer with the game...and you're even around in the holidays: Hidden inside chocolates you warm us when we're stuck in the midst of endless family gatherings. Yet lately, I've been wondering about your intentions.

You see, I want to believe that you have my best interests at heart, but I feel that your influence has led to unwise consequences, briefed below for your review:

1. Phone calls: While I agree with you that communication is important, I question the suggestion that any conversation of substance or necessity occurs at 5 a.m.

2. Eating: Now, you know I love a good meal and, though cooking is far from my specialty, why you suggested that I eat a kebab with chili sauce coupled with a pot noodle and some stale crisps (washed down with chocolate masque and topped off with a Kit Kat) is beyond me. Eclectic eater I am, but I think you went a bit too far this time.

3. Clumsiness: Unless you're subtly trying to tell me I need to do yoga more to increase my balance, I see NO need to hammer the issue home by causing me to fall down the stairs. Completely unnecessary. Similarly, it should never take me more than 30 seconds to get the front door key into the lock.

4. Pictures: This is a blessing in disguise, as it can often clarify the last point below, but the following costumes are heretofore banned from being placed

on my head in public: Indian Wigs, Sombreros, Bows, Ties, Boxes, upside-down cups, inflatable balloon animals, traffic cones, bras.

5. Beer Goggles: If I think I may know him/her from somewhere, I most likely do not. PLEASE do not request that I go over and see if in fact, I do actually know that person. This is similar to the old "Hey, you're in my class" syndrome circa 1996 at SU, and should heretofore be rendered illegal. Coupled with this is the phrase "Let's shag." While I may be thinking this, please reinstate the brain-to-mouth block that would keep this thought from being a statement, especially in public.

6. Please also refrain from changing ugly to pretty as I have blamed you several times for the ugliness I wake-up to and don't wanna do that again. Further, the subsequent hangovers have GOT to stop. Now, I know a little penance for our previous evenings' debauchery may be in order, but the 2 pm Hangover Immobility is completely unacceptable. I ask that if the proper steps are proactively taken on my part (i.e. water, vitamin B, bread products, aspirin) prior to going to bed/passing out facedown on the kitchen floor with a bag of popcorn, the hangover should be quite minimal and no way interfere with my daily Saturday or Sunday (or any day, for that matter) activities. Come on now, it's only fair-you do your part, I'll do mine.

Alcohol, I have enjoyed our relationship for some years now, and want to ensure that we remain on good terms. You've been the invoker of great stories, the provocation for much laughter, and the needed companion when we just don't know what to do with the extra money in our pockets. In order to continue this relationship, I ask that you carefully review my grievances above and address them immediately. I will look for an answer no later than Thursday at 9 pm on your possible solutions and hopefully we can continue this fruitful partnership.

Thank you.

Too Late

A man came home from work, sat down in his favorite chair, turned on the TV, and said to his wife, "Quick, bring me a beer before it starts."

She looked a little puzzled, but brought him beer. When he finished it, he said, "Quick, bring me another beer It's gonna start."

This time she looked a little angry, but brought him beer. When it was gone he said, "Quick, another beer before it starts."

"That's it!!" She blew her top! "You bastard! You waltz in here, flop your fat ass down, don't even say hello to me and then expect me to run around like your slave. Don't you realize that I cook and clean and wash and iron all day long?"

The husband sighed, "Shit, it started...."

Speak Engrish

A missionary who had spent years showing a tribe of natives how to farm and build things to be self-sufficient gets the word that he is to return home. He realizes that the one thing he never taught the natives was how to speak English, so he takes the chief and starts walking in the forest.

He points to a tree and says to the chief, "This is a tree." The chief looks at the tree and grunts, "Tree." The missionary is pleased with the response.

They walk a little farther and the padre points to a rock and says, "This is a rock." Hearing this, the chief looks and grunts, "Rock." The padre is really getting enthusiastic about the results when he hears a rustling in the bushes. As he peeks over the top, he sees a couple in the midst of heavy sexual activity. The padre is really flustered and quickly says, "Riding a bike."

The chief looks at the couple briefly, pulls out his blowgun and kills them. The padre goes ballistic and yells at the chief that he has spent years teaching the tribe how to be civilized and kind to each other, so how could he just kill these people in cold blood that way?

The chief replied, "My bike!"

Mongolian VD

An American tourist goes on a trip to China. While in China, he is very sexually promiscuous and does not use a condom all the time. A week after arriving back home in the States, he wakes one morning to find his penis covered with bright green and purple spots. Horrified, he immediately goes to see a doctor. The doctor, never having seen anything like this before, orders some tests and tells the man to return in two days for the results. The man returns a couple of days later and the doctor says, "I've got bad news for you. You've contracted Mongolian VD. It's very rare and almost unheard of here. We know very little about it."

The man looks a little perplexed and says: "Well, give me a shot or something and fix me up, Doc." The doctor answers: "I'm sorry, there's no known cure. We're going to have to amputate your penis". The man screams in horror, "Absolutely not! I want a second opinion". The doctor replies: "Well, it's your choice. Go ahead if you want, but surgery is your only choice."

The next day, the man seeks out a Chinese doctor, figuring that he'll know more about the disease.

The Chinese doctor examines his penis and proclaims: "Ah, yes, Mongolian VD. Vely lare disease."

The guy says to the doctor: "Yeah, yeah, I already know that, but what we can do? My American doctor wants to operate and amputate my penis!"

The Chinese doctor shakes his head and laughs, "Stupid Amelican docta, always want to opelate. Make mole money, that way. No need to opelate!"

"Oh, Thank God!" the man replies.

"Yes", says the Chinese doctor. "You no wolly! Wait two weeks. Dick fall off by itself! You save money."

Make an Appointment

A Scotsman goes to the dentist and asks how much it is for an extraction. "$85 for an extraction sir" was the dentists reply. "Och, huv ye nay got unythin cheaper?" replies the Scotsman getting agitated.

"But that's the normal charge for an extraction sir," said the dentist.

"What aboot if ye didnae use uny anaesthetic?" asked the Scotsman hopefully.

"Well it's highly unusual sir, but if that's what you want, I suppose I can do it for $70," said the dentist.

"Hmmmm, what aboot if ye used one of ye dentist trainees and still wi'oot anesthetic," said the Scotsman.

"Well it's possible but they are only training and I can't guarantee their level of professionalism and it'll be a lot more painful, but I suppose in that case we can bring the price down to say $40," said the dentist.

"Och that's still a bit much, how aboot if ye make it a training session and have yer student do the extraction and the other students watchin and learnin," said the Scotsman hopefully.

"Hmmmmm, well OK it'll be good for the students I suppose, I'll charge you only $5 in that case," said the dentist.

"Wonderful, it's a deal!" said the Scotsman. "Can ye book the wife in for next Tuesday?"

The Nymphomaniac

A man boarded an aircraft at London's Heathrow Airport and taking his seat as he settled in he noticed a very beautiful woman boarding the plane. He realised she was heading straight toward his seat and bingo! she took the seat right beside him. Eager to strike up a conversation, he blurted out, "Business trip or vacation?"

She turned, smiled enchantingly and said, "Business. I'm going to the annual nymphomaniac convention in the United States." He swallowed hard. Here was the most gorgeous woman he had ever seen sitting next to him, and she was going to a meeting for nymphomaniacs! Struggling to maintain his composure, he calmly asked, "What's your business role at this convention?" "Lecturer," she responded. "I use my experience to debunk some of the popular myths about sexuality." "Really!" he smiled. "What myths are those?"

"Well," she explained, "one popular myth is that

African-American men are the most well endowed when, in fact, it's the Native American Indian who is most likely to possess that trait. Another popular myth is that French men are the best lovers, when actually it is the men of Greek descent. We have also found that the best potential lovers in all categories are the Irish" Suddenly, the woman became uncomfortable and blushed. "I'm sorry," she said. "I really shouldn't be discussing this with you, I don't even know your name!"

"Tonto," the man said. "Tonto Papadopoulos, but my friends call me Paddy."

The Man Code

1. Under no circumstances may two men share an umbrella.
2. Any man who brings a camera to a bachelor party may be legally killed and eaten by his fellow partygoers.
3. When you are queried by a buddy's wife, girlfriend, mother, father, priest, shrink, dentist, accountant, or dog walker, you need not and should not provide any useful information whatsoever as to his whereabouts. You are permitted to deny his very existence.
4. Unless he murdered someone in your immediate family, you must bail a friend out of jail within 12 hours.
5. You may exaggerate any anecdote told in a bar by 50% without recrimination; beyond that, anyone within earshot is allowed to call bullshit! (Exception: When trying to pick up a girl, the allowable exaggeration rate rises to 400%)

6. If you've known a guy for more than 24 hours, his sister and immediate family is off-limits forever.

7. The minimum amount of time you have to wait for another guy who's running late is five minutes. For a girl, you are required to wait 10 minutes for every point of hotness she scores on the classic 1-10 babe scale.

8. Complaining about the brand of free beer in a buddy's refrigerator is forbidden. You may gripe if the temperature is unsuitable.

9. No man is ever required to buy a birthday present for another man. In fact, even remembering a friend's birthday is strictly optional and slightly gay.

10. Agreeing to distract the ugly friend of a hot babe that your buddy is trying to hook up with is your legal duty. Should you get carried away with your good deed and end up having sex with the beast, your pal is forbidden to speak of it, even at your bachelor party.

11. Before dating a buddy's ex, you are required to ask his permission and he in return is required to grant it.

12. Women who claim they "love to watch sports" must be treated as spies until they demonstrate knowledge of the game and the ability to pick a buffalo wing clean.

13. The universal compensation for buddies who help you move is beer.

14. When stumbling upon other guys watching a sports event, you may always ask the score of the game in progress, but you may never ask who's playing.

15. When your girlfriend/wife expresses a desire to fix her whiney friend up with your pal, you may give her the go-ahead only if you'll be able to warn your buddy and give him time to prepare excuses about joining the priesthood.

16. It is permissible to consume a fruity chick drink only when you're sunning on a tropical beach...and it's delivered by a topless supermodel...and it's free.

17. Unless you're in prison, never fight naked.

18. Never laugh at your buddy's manhood size.

19. A man in the company of a hot, suggestively dressed woman must remain sober enough to fight.

20. If a buddy is outnumbered, out-manned, or too drunk to fight, you must jump into the fight. (Exception: If within the last 24 hours his actions have caused you to think, "What this guy needs is a good ass-whoopin," then you may sit back and enjoy.)

21. Phrases that may not be uttered to another man while weightlifting:
    "Yeah, baby, push it!"
    "C'mon, give me one more! Harder!"
    "Another set and we can hit the showers."
    "Nice ass, are you a Sagittarius?"

22. If you compliment a guy on his six-pack, you better be referring to his beer.

23. Never join your girlfriend/wife in dissing a buddy, except when she's withholding sex pending your response.

24. Never talk to a man in the bathroom unless you're on equal footing: both urinating or both waiting in line. In all other situations, a nod is all the conversation you need.

25. If a buddy is already singing along to a song in the car, you may not, unless you are gay.
26. If you pass this on to a woman, you are breaking the ultimate man code.

Tricky Neighbor

A man is getting into the shower just as his wife is finishing up her shower when the doorbell rings. After a few seconds of arguing over which one should go and answer the doorbell, the wife gives up, quickly wraps herself up in a towel and runs downstairs. When she opens the door, there stands Bob, the next-door neighbor.

Before she says a word, Bob says, "I'll give you $800 to drop that towel that you have on" After thinking for a moment, the woman drops her towel and stands naked in front of Bob. After a few seconds, Bob hands her 800 dollars and leaves. Confused, but excited about her good fortune, the woman wraps back up in the towel and goes back upstairs. When she gets back to the bathroom, her husband asks from the shower, "Who was that?"

"It was Bob the next door neighbor," she replies. "Great!" the husband says, "Did he say anything about the $800 he owes me?"

Poor Dave

Dave works hard at the plant and spends most evenings bowling or playing basketball at the gym. His wife thinks he is pushing himself too hard, so for his birthday she takes him to a local strip club.

The doorman at the club greets them and says, "Hey, Dave! How ya doin?" His wife is puzzled and asks if he's been to this club before. "Oh no," says Dave. "He's on my bowling team."

When they are seated, a waitress asks Dave if he'd like his usual and brings over a Budweiser. His wife is becoming increasingly uncomfortable and says, "How did she know that you drink Budweiser?" "She's in the Ladies' Bowling League, honey. We share lanes with them."

A stripper then comes over to their table, throws her arms around Dave, starts to rub herself all over him and says "Hi Davey. Want your usual table dance, big boy?"

Dave's wife, now furious, grabs her purse and storms out of the club. Dave follows and spots her getting into a cab. Before she can slam the door, he jumps in beside her. Dave tries desperately to explain how the stripper must have mistaken him for someone else, but his wife is having none of it. She is screaming at him at the top of her lungs, calling him every four-letter word in the book.

The cabby turns his head and says, "Looks like you picked up a real bitch tonight, Dave."

That's My Boy!

Four men went golfing one day. Once on the course, three of them headed to the first tee and the fourth went into the clubhouse to take care of the bill.

The three men started talking, bragging about their sons. The first man told the others, "My son is a homebuilder and he is so successful that he gave a friend a new home for free."

The second man said, "My son was a car salesman and now he owns a multi-line dealership. He's so successful that he gave a friend a new Mercedes, with all the extras."

The third man, not wanting to be outdone, bragged, "My son is a stockbroker and he's doing so well that he gave his friend an entire stock portfolio."

The fourth man joined them on the tee after a few minutes of taking care of business. The first man mentioned, "We are just talking about our sons. How is yours doing?"

The fourth man replied, "Well, my son is gay and dances in a gay bar." The three friends looked down at the grass and sniggered.

The fourth man carried on, "Admittedly I'm not totally thrilled about the dancing job, but he must be doing pretty good. His last three boyfriends gave him a house, a brand new Mercedes, and a stock portfolio."

Lots of Blondes

A blind man enters a ladies bar by mistake. He finds his way to a bar stool and orders a drink. After sitting there for a while, he yells to the bartender, "Hey, you wanna hear a blonde joke?" The bar immediately falls absolutely quiet. In a very deep, husky voice, the woman next to him says, "Before you tell that joke, sir, you should know five things:

1. The bartender is a blonde girl.
2. The bouncer is a blonde gal.
3. I'm a 6 feet tall, 200 pound blonde woman with a black belt in karate.
4. The woman sitting next to me is blonde and is a professional weightlifter.
5. The lady to your right is a blonde and is a professional wrestler.

Now think about it seriously, Mister. Do you still wanna tell that joke? The blind man thinks for a second, shakes his head, and declares, "Nah, not if I'm gonna have to explain it five times"

New Watch

A very confident James Bond walks into a bar and takes a seat next to a very attractive woman. He gives her a quick glance, then casually looks at his watch for a moment. The woman notices this and asks, "Is your date running late?"

"No", he replies, "Q's just given me this state-of-the-art watch and I was just testing it."

The intrigued woman says, "A state-of-the-art watch? What's so special about it?"

Bond explains, "It uses alpha waves to talk to me telepathically."

The lady says, "What's it telling you now?"

"Well, it says you're not wearing any knickers...."

The woman giggles and replies, "Well it must be broken because I am wearing knickers!"

Bond tuts, taps his watch and says, "Damn thing's an hour fast."

The Test

A man is dating three women and wants to decide which to marry. He decides to give them a test. He gives each woman a present of $5000 and watches to see what they do with the money.

The first does a total makeover. She goes to a fancy beauty salon, gets her hair done, purchases new make-up and buys several new outfits, and dresses up very nicely for the man. She tells him that she has done this to be more attractive for him because she loves him so much. The man is impressed.

The second goes shopping to buy the man gifts. She gets him a new set of golf clubs, some new gizmos for his computer, and some expensive clothes. As she presents these gifts, she tells him that she has spent all the money on him because she loves him so much. Again, the man is impressed.

The third invests the money in the stock market. She earns several times the $5000. She gives him back his $5000 and reinvests the remainder in a joint account. She tells him that she wants to save for their future because she loves him so much. Obviously, the man was impressed.

The man thought for a long time about what each woman had done with the money. Then he married the one with the largest breasts.

Destiny

A woman and a man are involved in a car accident; it's a bad one. Both of their cars are totally demolished but amazingly neither of them are hurt. After they crawl out of their cars, the woman says, "So you're a man. That's interesting. I'm a woman. Wow, just look at our cars! There's nothing left, but we're unhurt. This must be a sign from God that we should meet and be friends and live together in peace for the rest of our days."

Flattered, the man replies, "Oh yes, I agree with you completely, this must be a sign from God!"

The woman continues, "And look at this, here's another miracle. My car is completely demolished but this bottle of wine didn't break. Surely God wants us to drink this wine and celebrate our good fortune." Then she hands the bottle to the man.

The man nods his head in agreement, opens it and drinks half the bottle and then hands it back to the woman.

The woman takes the bottle and immediately puts the cap back on, and hands it back to the man. The man asks, "Aren't you having any?"

The woman replies, "No. I think I'll just wait for the police...."

Boob Job

Two women were having lunch together, and discussing the merits of cosmetic surgery. The first woman says, "I need to be honest with you, I'm getting a boob job."

The second woman says "Oh that's nothing, I'm thinking of having my asshole bleached!"

To which the first replies, "Whoa...I just can't picture your husband as a blonde!"

Room for Rent

A businessman meets a beautiful girl and agrees to spend the night with her for $500. So they do. Before he leaves, he tells her that he does not have any cash with him, but he will have his secretary write a check and mail it to her, calling the payment "RENT FOR APARTMENT."

On the way to the office he regrets what he has done, realizing that the whole event was not worth the price. So he has his secretary send a check for $250 and enclosed the following typed note:

Dear Madam: Enclosed you will find a check in the amount of $250 for rent of your apartment. I am not sending the amount agreed upon, because when I rented the apartment, I was under the impression that:

1.   it had never been occupied
2.   that there was plenty of heat

3.   that it was small enough to make me feel cozy and at home.

However, I found out that it had been previously occupied, that there wasn't any heat, and that it was entirely too large.

Upon receipt of the note, the girl immediately returned the Check for $250 with the following note:

Dear Sir, First of all, I cannot understand how you expect a beautiful apartment to remain unoccupied indefinitely. As for the heat, there is plenty of it, if you know how to turn it on. Regarding the space, the apartment is indeed of regular size, but if you don't have enough furniture to fill it, please don't blame the landlady. Send the rent in full or we will be forced to contact your present landlady.

Respectfully Cheating

Jack and Betty are celebrating their 50th wedding anniversary. "Betty, I was wondering – have you ever cheated on me?" "Oh Jack, why would you ask such a question now? You don't want to ask that question..." "Yes, Betty, I really want to know. Please." "Well, all right. Yes, 3 times." "Three? When were they?" "Well, Jack, remember when you were 35 years old and you really wanted to start the business on your own and no bank would give you a loan? Remember how one day the bank president himself came over to the house and signed the loan papers, no questions asked?" "Oh, Betty, you did that for me! I respect you even more than ever, that you would do such a thing for me! So, when was number 2?" "Well, Jack, remember when you had that last heart attack and you were needing that very tricky operation, and no surgeon would touch you? Remember how Dr. DeBakey came all the way up here, to do the surgery himself, and then you were in good shape again?" "I can't believe it! Betty, I love that you should do such a thing for me, to save my life! I couldn't have a more wonderful wife. To do such a thing, you must really love me darling. I couldn't be more moved. When was number 3?" "Well, Jack, remember a few years ago, when you really wanted to be president of the golf club and you were 17 votes short?"

Mummy Knows Best

One afternoon a little girl returned from school, and announced that her friend had told her where babies come from. Amused, her mother replied, "Really, sweetie, Why don't you tell me all about it?"

The little girl explained, "Well...OK...Mummy and Daddy take off all of their clothes, and the Daddy's thingee sort of stands up, and then Mummy puts it in her mouth, and then it sort of explodes, and that's how you get babies."

Her mum shook her head, leaned over to meet her, eye to eye and said, "Oh, Darling, that's sweet, but that's not how you get babies. That's how you get jewellery!"

Social Security

A gentleman went to the social security office to apply for Social Security. The woman behind the counter asked him for his driver's license to verify his age. He looked in his pockets and realized he had left his wallet at home. He told the woman that he was very sorry but he seemed to have left his wallet at home. "I will have to go home and come back later."

The woman says, "Unbutton your shirt." So he opens his shirt revealing lots of curly silver hair.

She says, "That silver hair on your chest is proof enough for me" and she processed his Social Security application.

When he gets home, the man excitedly tells his wife about his experience at the Social Security office. She says, "You should have dropped your pants. You might have gotten disability too."

Extended Family

One Sunday morning, William burst into the living room and said, "Dad! Mom! I have some great news for you! I am getting married to the most beautiful girl in town. She lives a block away and her name is Susan.

After dinner, William's dad took him aside. "Son, I have to talk with you. Your mother and I have been married 30 years. She's a wonderful wife but she has not offered much excitement in the bedroom, so I used to fool around with women a lot. Susan is actually your half-sister, and I'm afraid you can't marry her."

William was heartbroken. After eight months he eventually started dating girls again. A year later he came home and proudly announced, "Diane said yes! We're getting married in June."

Again his father insisted on another private conversation and broke the sad news. "Diane is your half-sister too, William. I'm awfully sorry about this."

William was furious! He finally decided to go to his mother with the news. "Dad has done so much harm. I guess I'm never going to get married," he complained. "Every time I fall in love, Dad tells me the girl is my half-sister." His mother just shook her head. "Don't pay any attention to what he says. You can marry those girls, dear. He's not really your father."

Escaped Convict

A man escapes from prison where he has been for 15 years. He breaks into a house to look for money and guns and finds a young couple in bed. He orders the guy out of bed and ties him to a chair. While tying the girl to the bed he gets on top of her, kisses her neck, then gets up and goes into the bathroom. While he's in there, the husband tells his wife: "listen, this guy's an escaped convict, look at his clothes! He probably spent lots of time in jail and hasn't seen a woman in years. I saw how he kissed your neck. If he wants sex, don't resist, don't complain, do whatever he tells you. Satisfy him no matter how much he nauseates you. This guy is probably very dangerous. If he gets angry, he'll kill us. be strong, honey. I love you."

To which the wife responds: "He wasn't kissing my neck. He was whispering in my ear. He told me he was gay, thought you were cute, and asked if we had any Vaseline. I told him it was in the bathroom. Be strong honey. I love you too!!"

Using a Condom

Two old ladies were outside their nursing home, having a smoke when it started to rain. One of the ladies pulled out a condom, cut off the end, put it over her cigarette, and continued smoking.

Lady 1: What's that?
Lady 2: A condom. This way my cigarette doesn't get wet.
Lady 1: Where did you get it?

Lady 2: You can get them at any drugstore.

The next day, Lady 1 hobbles herself into the local drugstore and announces to the pharmacist that she wants a box of condoms. The guy, obviously embarrassed, looks at her kind of strangely (she is, after all, over 80 years of age), but very delicately asks what brand she prefers.

Lady 1: Doesn't matter son, as long as it fits a Camel.

The pharmacist fainted.

So That's What's Wrong with Men

Scientists have finally figured out what is wrong with men. The problem lies in the two halves of their brains - the left and the right. The left half has nothing right in it, and the right half has nothing left in it!

The Mexican Smuggler

Juan comes up to the Mexican border on his bicycle. He's got two large bags over his shoulders. The guard stops him and says, "What's in the bags?" "Sand," answered Juan. The guard says, "We'll just see about that get off the bike." The guard takes the bags and rips them apart; he empties them out and finds nothing in them but sand.

He detains Juan overnight and has the sand analyzed, only to discover that there is nothing but pure sand in the bags. The guard releases Juan, puts the sand into new bags, hefts them onto the man's shoulders, and lets him cross the border. A week later, the same thing happens. The guard asks, "What have you got?" "Sand," says Juan. The guard does his thorough examination and discovers that the bags contain nothing but sand. He gives the sand back to Juan, and Juan crosses the border on his bicycle. This sequence of events is repeated every day for three years. Finally, Juan doesn't show up one day and the guard meets him in a Cantina in Mexico. "Hey, Buddy," says the guard, "I know you are smuggling something. It's driving me crazy. It's all I think about...I can't sleep. Just between you and me, what are you smuggling?" Juan sips his beer and says, "Bicycles."

Last Requests

Mary Clancy goes up to Father O'Grady after his Sunday morning service, and she's in tears. He says, "So what's bothering you, Mary, my dear?"

She says, "Oh, Father, I've got terrible news. My husband passed away last night."

The priest says, "Oh, Mary, that's terrible. Tell me, Mary, did he have any last requests?"

She says, "That he did, Father."

The priest says, "What did he ask, Mary?"

She says, "He said, 'Please Mary, put down that damn gun...'"

Counting Cars

Five Englishmen in an Audi Quattro arrived at an Irish border checkpoint. Paddy the officer stops them and tells them: "It is illegal to put 5 people in a Quattro, Quattro means four."

"Quattro is just the name of the automobile," the Englishmen retorts disbelievingly.

"Look at the papers: this car is designed to carry five persons."

"You can not pull that one on me," replies Paddy "Quattro means four. You have five people in your car and you are therefore breaking the law."

The Englishmen replies angrily, "You idiot! Call your

supervisor over I want to speak to someone with more intelligence!"

"Sorry," responds Paddy. "Murphy is busy with 2 guys in a Fiat Uno."

It was an accident?

Brenda O'Malley is home making dinner, as usual, when Tim Finnegan arrives at her door."Brenda, may I come in?" he asks. "I've somethin' to tell ya."

"Of course you can come in, you're always welcome, Tim. But where's my husband?"

"That's what I'm here to be telling ya, Brenda. There was an accident down at the Guinness brewery..."

"Oh, God, no!" cries Brenda. "Please don't tell me..."

"I must, Brenda. Your husband Shamus is dead and gone. I'm sorry."

Finally, she looked up at Tim. "How did it happen, Tim?"

"It was terrible, Brenda. He fell into a vat of Guinness Stout and drowned."

"Oh, my dear Jesus! But you must tell me true, Tim. "Did he at least go quickly?"

"Well, no Brenda... no. Fact is, he got out three times to pee."

Going to Church

John O'Reilly hoisted his beer and said, "Here's to spending the rest of me life, between the legs of me wife!"

That won him the top prize at the pub for the best toast of the night! He went home and told his wife, Mary, "I won the prize for the best toast of the night." She said, "Aye, did ye now. And what was your toast?"

John said, "Here's to spending the rest of me life, sitting in church beside me wife." "Oh, that is very nice indeed, John!" Mary said.

The next day, Mary ran into one of John's drinking buddies on the street corner. The man chuckled leeringly and said, "John won the prize the other night at the pub with a toast about you, Mary." She said, "Aye, he told me, and I was a bit surprised meself. You know, he's only been there twice in the last four years. Once he fell asleep, and the other time I had to pull him by the ears to make him come."

A True Canadian

Two families move from India to Canada. When they arrive, the two fathers make each other a bet: In one year's time, whichever family has become more Canadian will win.

A year later when they meet again, the first guy says, "My son's playing hockey, I had Tim Horton's for breakfast and I'm on my way to pick up a two-four for tonight. How about you, eh?"

The second guy says, "Fuck you, Paki."

Fightin' Irish

Into a Belfast pub comes Paddy Murphy, looking like he'd just been run over by a train. His arm is in a sling, his nose is broken, his face is cut and bruised and he's walking with a limp. "What happened to you?" asks Sean, the bartender.

"Jamie O'Conner and me had a fight," says Paddy.

"That little shit, O'Conner," says Sean, "He couldn't do that to you, he must have had something in his hand."

"That he did," says Paddy, "a shovel is what he had, and a terrible lickin' he gave me with it."

"Well," says Sean, "you should have defended yourself, didn't you have something in your hand?"

"That I did," said Paddy. "Mrs. O'Conner's breast, and a thing of beauty it was, but useless in a fight."

Thank Heavens

An Irishman who had a little too much to drink is driving home from the city one night and, of course, his car is weaving violently all over the road. A cop pulls him over. "So," says the cop to the driver, "where have ya been?"

"Why, I've been to the pub of course," slurs the drunk.

"Well," says the cop, "it looks like you've had quite a few to drink this evening."

"I did all right," the drunk says with a smile.

"Did you know," says the cop, standing straight and folding his arms across his chest, "that a few intersections back, your wife fell out of your car?"

"Oh, thank heavens," sighs the drunk. "For a minute there, I thought I'd gone deaf."

Stranded on an Island

A ship sank in high seas and the following people got stranded on a beautiful deserted island in the middle of nowhere:

A. 2 Italian men and 1 Italian woman
B. 2 French men and 1 French woman
C. 2 German men and 1 German woman
D. 2 Greek men and 1 Greek woman
E. 2 Polish men and 1 Polish woman

F.   2 Mexican men and 1 Mexican woman

H.   2 American men and 1 American woman

I.   2 Indian men and 1 Indian woman

One month later, on various parts of the island, the following was observed:

A.   One Italian man killed the other Italian man for the Italian woman.

B.   The two French men and the French woman are living happily together.

C.   The two German men have a strict weekly schedule of when they alternate with the German woman.

D.   The two Greek men are sleeping together, and the Greek woman is cooking & cleaning for them.

E.   The two Polish men took a long look at the endless ocean and a long look at the Polish woman, and they started swimming.

F.   The two Mexican men are talking to all the other men on the island trying to sell them the Mexican woman.

H.   The two American men are contemplating suicide. The American woman is complaining about her body being her own, the true nature of feminism, how she can do everything that they can do, about the necessity of fulfillment, the equal division of the household chores, how her last boyfriend respected her opinion and treated her much better, and how her relationship with her mother is improving.

I.   The two Indian men are still waiting for someone to introduce them to the Indian woman.

Parking in Manhattan

A Chinese walks into a bank in New York City and asks for the loan officer. He tells the loan officer that he is going to Taiwan on business for two weeks and needs to borrow $5,000.

The bank officer tells him that the bank will need some form of security for the loan, so the Chinese hands over the keys to a new Ferrari parked on the street in front of the bank. He produces the title and everything checks out. The loan officer agrees to accept the car as collateral for the loan.

The bank's president and it's officers all enjoy a good laugh at the Chinese for using a $250,000 Ferrari as collateral against a $5,000 loan.

An employee of the bank then drives the Ferrari into the bank's underground garage and parks it there.

Two weeks later, the Chinese returns, repays the $5,000 and the interest, which comes to $15.41. The loan officer says, "Sir, we are very happy to have had your business, and this transaction has worked out very nicely, but we are a little puzzled. While you were away, we checked you out and found that you are a multi-millionaire. What puzzles us is, why would you bother to borrow $5,000?"

The Chinese replies: "Where else in New York City can I park my car for two weeks for only $15.41 and expect it to be there when I return?"

10 Things In Golf That Sound Dirty

1. Look at the size of his putter.
2. Oh shit, my shaft's all bent.
3. You really wacked the hell out of that sucker.
4. After 18 holes I can barely walk.

5. My hands are so sweaty I can't get a good grip.
6. Lift your head and spread your legs.
7. You have a nice stroke, but your follow through leaves a lot to be desired.
8. Just turn your back and drop it.
9. Hold up. I've got to wash my balls.
10. Damn, I missed the hole again.

Golf Fatality

A guy goes golfing with his girlfriend. As he tees off, she steps into ladies' teebox and gets hit in the head with his drive. She is pronounced D.O.A. and taken to the morgue. The coroner calls him in and says, "She definitely died from a blow to the head caused by the golf ball. But the only thing we can't understand is why was there a golf ball in her rectum?" "Oh," he replies, "that must have been my mulligan."

Things to think about

1. Who was the first person to look at a cow and say, "I think I'll squeeze these dangly things here, and drink whatever comes out?"
2. Who was the first one who thought that the white thing that came from a hen's butt looked edible?
3. Why do toasters always have a setting that burns the toast to a horrible crisp which no decent human being would eat?
4. Why is there a light in the fridge and not in the freezer?
5. Can a hearse carrying a corpse drive in the carpool lane?

6. If the professor on Gilligan's Island can make a radio out of coconut, why can't he fix a hole in a boat?

7. Why do people point to their wrist when asking for the time, but don't point to their crotch when they ask where the bathroom is?

8. Why does your OB-GYN leave the room when you get undressed if they are going to look up there anyway?

9. Why does goofy stand erect while Pluto remains on all fours? They're both dogs!

10. If Wile E. Coyote had enough money to buy all that Acme crap, why didn't he just buy dinner?

11. Why is a person that handles your money called a Broker?

12. If quizzes are quizzical, what are tests?

13. If corn oil is made from corn, and vegetable oil is made from vegetables, then what is baby oil made from?

14. If a man is talking in the forest, and no woman is there to hear him, is he still wrong?

15. Did you know that the Alphabet song and Twinkle, Twinkle Little Star have the same tune?

16. (Are you singing them both to really find out?)

17. Did you ever notice that when you blow in a dog's face, he gets mad at you, but when you take him on a car ride, he sticks his head out the window.

18. Why is it that when someone tells you that there are over a billion stars in the universe, you believe them, but if they tell you there is wet paint somewhere, you have to touch it to make sure?

19. Still singing? Try "bah bah black sheep" too!

Scary Thought

A cardiologist died and was given an elaborate funeral. A huge heart covered in flowers stood behind the casket during the service. Following the eulogy, the heart opened, and the casket rolled inside. The heart then closed, sealing the doctor in the beautiful heart forever.

At that point, one of the mourners burst into laughter. When all eyes stared at him, he said, "I'm sorry, I was just thinking of my own funeral...I'm a gynecologist."

That's when the proctologist fainted.

The Witty Truck Driver

A truck driver was driving along on the freeway. A sign comes up that reads "low bridge ahead." He tries to turn off but, before he knows it, the bridge is right there and he gets stuck under it. Cars are backed up for miles. Finally, a police car comes up. The cop gets out of his car and walks around to the truck driver, puts his hands on his hips and says, "Got stuck huh?" The truck driver says, "No, I was delivering this bridge and ran out of gas."

Golf Genie

A husband and wife, out enjoying a round of golf, were about to tee off on the third hole, which was lined with beautiful homes. The wife hit her shot and the ball began to slice - her shot was headed directly at a very large plate glass window. Much to her surprise, the ball smashed through the window and shattered it into a million pieces. They felt compelled to see what damage was done and drove off to see what happened. When they peeked inside the house, they found no one there. The husband called out and no one answered. Upon further investigation, they saw a small gentleman sitting on the couch with a turban on his head. The wife asked the man, "Do you live here?"

"No, someone just hit a ball through the window, knocked over the vase you see there, freeing me from that little bottle. I am so grateful!" he answered.

The wife asked, "Are you a genie?" "Oh, why yes I am. In fact, I am so grateful I will grant you two wishes, and the third I will keep for myself," the man replied.

The husband and wife agreed on two wishes - one was for a scratch handicap for the husband, to which the wife readily agreed. The other was for an income of $1,000,000 per year forever.

The genie nodded his head and said, "Done!" The genie now said, "For my wish, I would like to have my way with your wife. I have not been with a woman for many years, and after all, I made you a scratch golfer and a millionaire."

The husband and wife agreed. After the genie and wife were finished, the genie asked the wife, "How long have you been married?" To which she responded, "Three years." The genie then asked, "How old is your husband?" To which she replied, "31 years old" The genie then asked, "And how long has he believed in this genie crap?"

Accident Report

This man was in an accident at work, so he filled out an insurance claim. The insurance company contacted him and asked for more information. This was his response: "I am writing in response to your request for additional information, for block number 3 of the accident reporting form. I put 'poor planning' as the cause of my accident. You said in your letter that I should explain more fully and I trust the following detail will be sufficient.

I am an amateur radio operator and on the day of the accident, I was working alone on the top section of my new 80-foot tower. When I had completed my work, I discovered that I had, over the course of several trips up the tower, brought up about 300 pounds of tools and spare hardware. Rather than carry the now unneeded tools and material down by hand, I decided to lower the items down in a small barrel by using the pulley attached to the gin pole at the top of the tower. Securing the rope at ground level, I went to the top of the tower and loaded the tools and material into the barrel. Then I went back to the ground and untied the rope, holding it tightly to ensure a slow decent of the 300 pounds of tools.

"You will note in block number 11 of the accident reporting form that I weigh only 155 pounds. Due to my surprise of being jerked off the ground so suddenly, I lost my presence of mind and forgot to let go of the rope. Needless to say, I proceeded at a rather rapid rate of speed up the side of the tower. In the vicinity of the 40-foot level, I met the barrel coming down. This explains my fractured skull and broken collarbone. Slowed only slightly, I continued my rapid ascent, not stopping until the fingers of my right hand were two knuckles deep into the pulley. Fortunately, by this time, I had regained my presence of mind and was able to hold onto the rope in spite of my pain. At approximately the same time, however, the barrel of tools hit the ground and the bottom fell out of the barrel. Devoid of the weight of the tools, the barrel now weighed approximately 20 pounds. I refer you again to my weight in block number 11. As you might imagine, I began a rapid descent down the side of the tower. In the vicinity of the 40-foot level, I met the barrel coming up. This accounts for the two fractured ankles, and the lacerations of my legs and lower body. The encounter with the barrel slowed me enough to lessen my injuries when I fell onto the pile of tools and, fortunately, only three vertebrae were cracked. I am sorry to report, however, that as I lay there on the tools, in pain, unable to stand and watching the empty barrel 80 feet above me, I again lost my presence of mind. I let go of the rope."

Fall-Down Drunk

A man, whose level of drunkenness was bordering on the absurd, stood up to leave a bar and fell flat on his face. "Maybe all I need is some fresh air," thought the man as he crawled outside. He tried to stand up again, but fell face first into the mud. "Screw it," he thought. "I'll just crawl home."

The next morning, his wife found him on the doorstep asleep. "You went out drinking last night, didn't you?" she said.

"Uh, yes," he said sheepishly. "How did you know?"

"You left your wheelchair at the bar again."

Two Brothers

There were two brothers. One was very good and tried to always live right and be helpful. His brother on the other hand was bad and did all the things that men should not do in life and didn't care who he hurt. The bad brother died. He was still missed by his brother since he loved him despite his ways. Finally, years later, the good brother died and went to Heaven. Everything was beautiful and wonderful there, and he was very happy.

One day he asked God where his brother was, as he hadn't seen him there. God said that he was sorry but his brother lived a terrible life and went to Hell instead.

The good brother then asked God if there was any way for him to see his brother. So God gave him the power of vision to see into Hell and there was his brother. He was sitting on a bench with a keg of beer under one arm and a gorgeous blonde on the other.

Confused, the good brother said to God, "I am so happy that you let me into Heaven with you. It is so beautiful here and I love it. But I don't understand, if my brother was bad enough to go to Hell, why does he have the keg of beer and a gorgeous blonde? It hardly seems like a punishment."

God said unto him, "Things are not always as they seem, my son. The keg has a hole in it; the blonde doesn't."

Useless

A cowboy was herding his herd in a remote pasture when suddenly a brand-new BMW advanced out of a dust cloud towards him. The driver, a young man in a Brioni suit, Gucci shoes, Ray Ban sunglasses and YSL tie, leans out the window and asks the cowboy, "If I tell you exactly how many cows and calves you have in your herd, will you give me a calf?"

The cowboy looks at the man, obviously a yuppie, then looks at his peacefully grazing herd and calmly answers, "Sure. Why not?"

The yuppie parks his car, whips out his Dell notebook computer, connects it to his AT&T cell phone, surfs to a NASA page on the Internet, where he calls up a GPS satellite navigation system to get an exact fix on this location which he then feeds to another NASA satellite that scans the area in an ultra-high-resolution photo. The young man then opens the digital photo in Adobe Photoshop and exports it to an image processing faculty in Hamburg, Germany. Within seconds, he receives an email on his Palm Pilot that the image has been processed and the data stored. He then accesses a MS_SQL database through an ODBC connected Excel spreadsheet with hundreds of complex formulas. He uploads all of this data via an email on his Blackberry and, after a few minutes, receives a response. Finally, he prints out a full-color 150 page report on this hi-tech, miniaturized HP LaserJet printer and at last turns to the cowboy and says, "You have exactly 1586 cows and calves."

"That's right. Well, I guess you can take one of my calves," says the cowboy. He watches the young man select one of the animals and looks on amused as the young man stuffs it into the trunk of this car.

Then the cowboy says to the young man, "Hey, if I can tell you exactly what your business is, will you give me back my calf?"

The young man thinks about it for a second and then says, "Okay, why not?"

"You're a consultant." says the cowboy.

"Wow! That's correct," says the yuppie, "but how did you guess that?"

"No guessing required." answered the cowboy. "You showed up here even though nobody called you; you want to get paid for an answer I already knew to a question I never asked; and you don't know anything about my business. Now, give me back my dog."

Don't Kick the Animals

A boy awoke and wanted breakfast so he told his mother. She said, "Not until you feed the animals."

The boy went outside and said to the chicken, "I don't feel like feeding you today." So he kicked the chicken. He did the same with the cow and the pig. The boy then went back into the house and told his mother he was hungry. His mother said, "I saw you kick the chicken so you're not getting any eggs, I saw you kick the cow so you're not getting any milk and I saw kick the pig so you're not getting any bacon."

Just then the boy's father walked down the steps and tripped over and kicked the cat and the boy said, "Mom should I tell him?"

The First Affair

There was a middle-age couple that had two stunningly beautiful teen-age daughters. The couple decided to try one last time for the son they always wanted. After months of trying, the wife became pregnant and, sure enough delivered a healthy baby boy nine months later. The joyful father rushed to the nursery to see his new son. He took one look and was horrified to find the ugliest child he had ever seen. He went to his wife and said that there was no way that he could be the father of the child. "Look at the two beautiful daughters I fathered," he cried. Then he gave her a stern look and asked, "Have you been fooling around on me?" The wife smiled sweetly and said, "Not this time."

The Second Affair

A mortician was working late one night. It was his job to examine the dead bodies before they were sent off to be buried or cremated. As he examined the body of Mr Schwartz, he made an amazing discovery - Schwartz had the longest penis he had ever seen! "I'm sorry, Mr Schwartz," said the mortician, "but I can't send you off to be cremated with a tremendously huge penis like this. It has to be saved for posterity." And with that the coroner used his scalpel to remove the dead man's privates. The coroner stuffed his prize into a briefcase and took it home. The first person he showed was his wife. "I have something to show you that you won't believe," he said, opening his briefcase. "Oh, my God!" she screamed, "Schwartz is dead!"

The Third Affair

A woman was in bed with her lover when she heard her husband opening the front door. "Hurry!" she said. "Stand in the corner!" She quickly rubbed baby oil all over him and then she dusted him with talcum powder. "Don't move until I tell you to," she whispered. "Just pretend you're a statue." "What's this, honey?" the husband inquired as he entered the room. "Oh, it's just a statue," she replied nonchalantly. "The Smiths bought it for their bedroom. I liked it so much, I got one for us, too." No more was said about the statue, not even later that night when they went to sleep. Around 2 a.m., the husband got out of bed, went to the kitchen and returned a while later with a sandwich and a glass of milk. "Here," he said to the statue, "Eat something. I stood like an idiot at the Smiths' for three days, and nobody offered me as much as a glass of water."

The Fourth Affair

A man walks into a bar one night. He goes up to the bartender and asks for a beer. "Certainly, sir," replies the bartender. "That'll be one cent." "ONE CENT!" exclaims the customer. The barman replies, "Yes." So the guy glances over the menu and asks, "Could I have a nice juicy T-bone steak with chips, peas and a fried egg?" "Certainly, sir," replies the bartender, "but all that comes to real money." "How much money?" inquires the guy. "Four cents," the bartender replies. "FOUR cents!" exclaims the guy "Where's the guy who owns this place?" The bartender replies, "Upstairs with my wife." The guy asks, "What's he doing with your wife?" The bartender replies, "Same as I'm doing to his business."

The Fifth Affair

Jake was dying. His wife, Becky, was maintaining a candlelight vigil by his side. She held his fragile hand, tears running down her face. Her praying roused him from his slumber. He looked up and his pale lips began to move slightly. "My darling Becky," he whispered. "Hush, my love," she said. "Rest. Shhh, don't talk." He was insistent. "Becky," he said in his tired voice, "I have something I must confess to you." "There's nothing to confess," replied the weeping Becky. "Everything's all right. Go to sleep." "No, no, I must die in peace, Becky. I slept with your sister, your best friend, her best friend and your mother!" "I know," Becky whispered softly, "That's why I poisoned you."

The Sixth Affair

An elderly gent was invited to his old friend's home for dinner one evening. He was impressed by the way his buddy preceded every request to his wife with endearing terms - "Honey," "My Love," "Darling," "Sweetheart," "Pumpkin," etc. The couple had been married almost 70 years and, clearly, they were still very much in love. While the wife was in the kitchen, the man leaned over and said to his host, "I think it's wonderful that, after all these years, you still call your wife those loving pet names." The old man hung his head. "I have to tell you the truth," he said. I forgot her name about 10 years ago."

Delicacy

A big Texan cowboy stopped at a local restaurant following a day of drinking and roaming around in Mexico. While sipping his tequila, he noticed a sizzling, scrumptious looking platter being served at the next table. Not only did it look good, the smell was wonderful. He asked the waiter, "What is that you just served?"

The waiter replied, "Ah senor, you have excellent taste! Those are bull's testicles from the bull fight this morning, a delicacy!" The cowboy, though momentarily daunted, said "What the heck, I'm on vacation down here! Bring me an order!"

The waiter replied, "I am so sorry, senor. There is only one serving per day because there is only one bull fight each morning.

If you come early tomorrow and place your order, we will be sure to save you this delicacy"!

The next morning, the cowboy returned, placed his order, and then that evening he was served the one and only special delicacy of the day. After a few bites, and inspecting the contents of his platter, he called to the waiter and said, "These are delicious, but they are much, much smaller than the ones I saw you serve yesterday!"

The waiter shrugged his shoulders and replied, "Si, Senr. Sometimes the bull wins."

How to Shower Like a Woman

Take off clothing and place it in sectioned laundry hamper according to whites and coloured.

Walk to bathroom wearing long dressing gown.

If you see husband along the way, cover up any exposed areas.

Look at your womanly physique in the mirror - make mental note to do more sit-ups.

Get in shower.

Use face cloth, arm cloth, leg cloth, long loofah, wide loofah and pumice stone.

Wash hair once with cucumber and sage shampoo with 43 added vitamins.

Wash hair again to make sure it is clean.

Condition hair with grapefruit mint conditioner enhanced with natural avocado oil, leave on hair for 15 minutes.

Wash face with crushed apricot facial, scrub for 10 minutes until red.

Wash entire rest of body with gingernut and jaffa cake body wash.

Shave armpits and legs.

Turn off shower.

Squeegee off all wet surfaces in shower, spray mould spots with Tilex.

Get out off shower.

Dry with towel the size of a small country.

Wrap hair in super absorbent towel.

Check entire body for spots, tweeze hairs.

Return to bedroom wearing long dressing gown and towel on head.

If you see husband along the way, cover any exposed areas.

How to Shower Like a Man

Take off clothes while sitting on the edge of the bed.

Leave in a pile.

Walk naked to the bathroom.

If you see wife along the way, shake knob at her making woo-hoo sound.

Look at manly physique in the mirror.

Admire size of your knob and scratch your ass.

Get in the shower.

Wash your face.

Wash your armpits.

Blow your nose in your hands and let the water rinse them off.

Make fart noises (real or artificial) and laugh at how loud they sound in the shower.

Spend majority of time washing privates and surrounding area.

Wash your butt leaving those coarse hairs stuck on the soap.

Shampoo hair.

Make shampoo mohawk.

Pee.

Rinse off and get out of shower.

Partially dry-off.

Fail to notice water on floor.

Admire knob size in mirror again.

Leave shower door open, wet mat on floor, light and fan on.

Return to bedroom with towel around waist.

If you pass wife, pull off towel, shake knob at her and make woo-hoo noise again.

Throw wet towel on bed

Everything I Want

A married couple is driving along a highway doing a steady forty miles per hour. The wife is behind the wheel. Her husband suddenly looks across at her and speaks in a clear voice. "Darling," he says. "I know we've been married for twenty years, but I want a divorce."

The wife says nothing, keeps looking at the road ahead but slowly increases her speed to 45 mph. the husband speaks again. "I don't want you to try and talk me out of it,"he says, "because I've been having an affair with your best friend, and she's a far better lover than you are."

Again the wife stays quiet, but grips the steering wheel more tightly and slowly increases the speed to 55. He pushes his luck. "I want the house," he says insistently. Speed up to 60. "I want the car, too," he continues. Speed up to 65 mph. "And," he says, "I'll have the bank accounts, all the credit cards and the boat." The car slowly starts veering towards a massive concrete bridge. This makes him a wee bit nervous, so he asks her: "Isn't there anything you want?"

The wife at last replies - in a quiet and controlled voice. "No, I've got everything I need," she says. "Oh, really?" he inquires, "so what have you got?" Just before they slam into the wall at 75 mph, the wife turns to him and smiles. "The airbag."

Lessons Learned

A Bihari hat seller who was passing by a forest decided to take a nap under one of the trees, so he left his whole basket of hats by the side.

A few hours later, he woke up and realized that all his hats were gone. He looked up and to his surprise, the tree was full of monkeys and they had taken all his hats. The Bihari sits down and thinks of how he can get the hats down. While thinking he started to scratch his head. The next moment, the monkeys were doing the same. Next, he took down his own hat, the monkeys did exactly the same. An idea came to him, he took his hat and threw it on the floor and the monkeys did that too. So he finally managed to get all his hats back.

Fifty years later, his grandson, Laloo, also became a hat seller and had heard this monkey story from his grandfather. One day, just like his grandfather, he passed by the same forest. It was very hot, and he took a nap under the same tree and left he hats on the floor. He woke up and realized that all his hats were taken by the monkeys on the tree. He remembered his grandfather's words, started scratching his head and the monkeys followed. He took down his hat and fanned himself and again the monkeys followed. Now, very convinced of his grandfather's idea, Laloo threw his hat on the floor but to his surprise, the monkeys still held on to all the hats. Then one monkey climbed down the tree, grabbed the hat on the floor, gave him a slap and said, "You think only you have a grandfather?"

Solved . . . finally

A chicken and an egg are lying in bed. The chicken is leaning against the headboard smoking a cigarette with a satisfied smile on its face. The egg, looking a bit pissed off, grabs the sheet, rolls over and says, "Well, I guess we finally answered THAT question."

Old Lady Speeding

An older lady gets pulled over for speeding.

Older Woman: Is there a problem, Officer?

Officer: Ma'am, you were speeding.

Older Woman: Oh, I see.

Officer: Can I see your license please?

Older Woman: I'd give it to you but I don't have one.

Officer: Don't have one?

Older Woman: Lost it, 4 years ago for drunk driving.

Officer: I see...Can I see your vehicle registration papers please.

Older Woman: I can't do that.

Officer: Why not?

Older Woman: I stole this car.

Officer: Stole it?

Older Woman: Yes, and I killed and hacked up the owner.

Officer: You what?

Older Woman: His body parts are in plastic bags in the trunk if you want to see.

The Officer looks at the woman and slowly backs away to his car and calls for back up. Within minutes 5 police cars circle the car. A senior officer slowly approaches the car, clasping his half-drawn gun.

Officer 2: Ma'am, could you step out of your vehicle please! The woman steps out of her vehicle.

Older woman: Is there a problem sir?

Officer 2: One of my officers told me that you have stolen this car and murdered the owner.

Older Woman: Murdered the owner?

Officer 2: Yes, could you please open the trunk of your car, please.

The woman opens the trunk, revealing nothing but an empty trunk.

Officer 2: Is this your car, ma'am?

Older Woman: Yes, here are the registration papers.

The officer is quite stunned.

Officer 2: One of my officers claims that you do not have a driving license.

The woman digs into her handbag and pulls out a clutch purse and hands it to the officer. The officer examines the license. He looks quite puzzled.

Officer 2: Thank you ma'am, one of my officers told me you didn't have a license, that you stole this car, and that you murdered and hacked up the owner.

Older Woman: Bet the liar told you I was speeding, too.

No Dancing

A modern Islamic couple, preparing for a religious wedding meets with their Mullah for counseling. The Mullah asks if they have any last questions before they leave. The man asks, "We realize it's a tradition in Islam for men to dance with men, and women to dance with women. But, at our wedding reception, we'd like your permission to dance together."

"Absolutely not," says the Mullah. "It's immoral. Men and women always dance separately."

"So after the ceremony I can't even dance with my own wife?"

"No," answered the Mullah, "It's forbidden in Islam."

"Well, okay," says the man, "What about sex? Can we finally have sex?"

"Of course!" replies the Mullah, "Sex is OK within marriage, to have children!"

"What about different positions?" asks the man.

"No problem," says the Mullah.

"Woman on top?" the man asks.

"Sure," says the Mullah. "Go for it!"

"Doggy style?"

"Sure!"

"On the kitchen table?"

"Yes, yes!"

"Can we do it with all my four wives together on rubber sheets with a bottle of hot oil, a couple of vibrators, leather harnesses, a bucket of honey and a porno video?"

"You may indeed."

"Can we do it standing up?"

"No." says the Mullah."

"Why not?" asks the man. "Because that could lead to dancing."

A Great Weekend

A man walked into a jewellery shop late one Friday with a beautiful young lady at his side.

"I'm looking for a special ring for my girlfriend," he said.

The shop owner looked through his stock and took out a lovely ring priced at $1,000.

"I don't think you understand, I want something very unique," the customer said.

At that, the shop owner went to get his special stock

from the safe. "Here's a stunning ring at just $8,000."

The girl's eyes sparkled and the man said that he would take it.

"How are you paying?"

"I'll pay by check, but of course you will want to make sure everything is in order at the bank, so I'll write the check and you can phone the bank tomorrow. I'll pick up the ring on Monday."

Monday morning a very pissed-off shop owner phoned the man.

"You bloody cheater! There's no money in that account!"

"I know, but can you imagine what a fantastic weekend I had?"

The Five Secrets of a Perfect Relationship

1. It is important to find a woman who cooks, cleans up and has a job.
2. It is important to find a woman who can make you laugh.
3. It is important to find a woman who you can trust and who doesn't lie to you.
4. It is important to find a woman who is good in bed and who likes to be with you.
5. It is very, very, very important that these four women don't know each other.

Three Extra Inches

A man enters his favorite restaurant and sits at his regular table. Looking around, he notices a gorgeous woman sitting at a table nearby, all alone. He calls the waiter over and asks him to send her their most expensive bottle of merlot, knowing that if she accepts it, she is his.

The waiter gets the bottle and takes it over to the girl saying "This is from the gentleman over there," indicating to him.

She regards the wine coolly for a second and decides to send a note over to the man. The waiter, who was lingering for a response, took the note from her and conveyed it to the gentleman.

The note read: "For me to accept this bottle, you need to have a Mercedes in your garage, a million dollars in the bank and seven inches in your pants."

After reading the note, the man decided to compose one of his own in return. He handed it to the waiter and instructed him to deliver it to the lady.

It read: "For your information, I happen to have a Ferrari Testarossa, a BMW 850iL and a Mercedes 560SEL in my garage; plus I have over twenty million dollars in the bank. But, not even for a woman as beautiful as you would I cut off three inches. Just send the bottle back."

Geography of a Woman

Between 18 and 20, a woman is like Africa: half-discovered, half-wild, naturally beautiful with fertile deltas.

Between 21 and 30, a woman is like America: well-developed and open to trade, especially for someone with cash.

Between 31 and 35, she is like India: very hot, relaxed and convinced of her own beauty.

Between 36 and 40, a woman is like France: gently aging but still a warm and desirable place to visit.

Between 41 and 50, she is like Yugoslavia: lost the war, haunted by past mistakes. Massive reconstruction is necessary.

Between 51 and 60, she is like Russia: very wide and borders are unpatrolled. The frigid climate keeps people away.

Between 61 and 70, a woman is like Mongolia: a glorious and all-conquering past but alas, no future.

After 70, a woman is like Afghanistan: everyone knows where it is, but no one wants to go there.

The Geography of a Man

Between 15 and 90, a man is like Zimbabwe: ruled by a dick.

Trading Places

A man was sick and tired of going to work every day while his wife stayed home. He wanted her to see what he went through so he prayed: "Dear Lord: I go to work every day and put in 8 hours while my wife merely stays at home. I want her to know what I go through, so please allow her body to switch with mine for a day. Amen."

God, in his infinite wisdom, granted the man's wish. The next morning, sure enough, the man awoke as a woman.

He arose, cooked breakfast for his mate, awakened the kids, Set out their school clothes, fed them breakfast, packed their lunches, Drove them to school, came home and picked up the dry cleaning, took it to the cleaners And stopped at the bank to make a deposit, went grocery shopping, Then drove home to put away the groceries, Paid the bills and balanced the checkbook. He cleaned the cat's litter box and bathed the dog. Then it was already 1 p.m. and he hurried to make the beds, do the laundry, vacuum, dust, and sweep and mop the kitchen floor. Ran to the school to pick up the kids and got into an argument with them on the way home. Set out milk and cookies and got the kids organized to do their homework, then set up the ironing board and watched TV while he did the ironing. At 4:30 he began peeling potatoes and washing vegetables for salad, breaded the pork chops and snapped fresh beans for supper. After supper, he cleaned the kitchen, ran the dishwasher, folded laundry, bathed the kids, and put them to bed. At 9 p.m. he was exhausted and, though his daily chores weren't finished, he went to bed where he was expected to make love, which he managed to get through without complaint.

The next morning, he awoke and immediately knelt by the bed and said, Lord, I don't know what I was thinking. I was so wrong to envy my wife's being able to stay home all day. Please, oh please, let us trade back."

The Lord, in his infinite wisdom, replied, "My son, I feel you have learned your lesson and I will be happy to change things back to the way they were. You'll just have to wait nine months, though. You got pregnant last night."

Better than Baghdad?

A rather desperate Paul Langmack, coach of the South Sydney Rabbitohs, gets wind of a potential new young recruit who lives in Iraq. The club has inspirational leader George Piggins catch a plane to war-torn Baghdad and track down the young boy. George risks life and limb dodging bombs, bullets and grenades but finally finds the boy and convinces him to come to Australia. He does a full pre-season, plays in all the practice matches and gets picked on the bench in first grade for the first premiership game of the year.

Ten minutes into the first half, Bryan Fletcher goes down with a severe knee injury. Langmack turns to the boy and says "This is it son, go into the second row and show us what you can do."

The boy proceeds to play the greatest debut game in NRL history. He scores two tries, tops the tackle count, and kicks the winning goal after the siren from on the sideline.

The Rabbits chair him off the ground and give him three cheers back in the rooms. Langmack tells the team what the boy from Iraq has been through and that he is a model lesson for all.

Langmack then pulls the boy aside and says "Go into my office son, ring your Mother and tell her what you did today".

He proceeds to do so. "Mum", he says down the phone, "Guess what I did today? "I don't care what you did today his Mother replies. "I tell you what happened here today," she goes on. "Your Dad was stabbed and robbed, the house was fire bombed, our car blown up, your sister raped and your brother's been abducted."

"Gee," says the boy. "I feel a bit responsible for what happened".

His Mother replies "So you should be, if it wasn't for you we would never have shifted to Sydney...."

Clocks in Heaven

A man died and went to heaven. As he stood in front of St. Peter at the Pearly Gates, he saw a huge wall of clocks behind him. Curious, he asked, "What are all those clocks?"

St. Peter answered, "Those are Lie-Clocks. Everyone on Earth has a Lie-Clock. Every time you lie, the hands on your clock will move."

"Oh," said the man, "and whose clock is that?"

"That is Mother Teresa's. The hands have never moved, indicating that she never told a lie."

"Incredible," said the man. "And whose clock is that one?" St. Peter responded, "That's Ray Charles' clock. The hands have moved twice, telling us that Ray told only two lies in his entire life."

Looking around, the man asked "Where is John Howard's clock?"

"In Jesus' office - he's using it as a ceiling fan."